SOMETHING GAINED

LARGE PRINT EDITION

ALSO BY C.K. CARR

Novels
Something Worth Having
Something Gained

Short Stories
Shelter From The Storm

Something
Gained

C.K. CARR

CHAPTER 1

Jackie's hand shook as she brought the lipstick to her mouth. She paused, closing her eyes against the wave of sorrow that washed through her. Her stomach clenched at the thought of what she was about to do, but she had to do it.

It was time. Past time. Dave had been gone for over a year.

She opened her sapphire-blue eyes and studied herself in the mirror for a long moment, her hand resting against the marble of the vanity. Dark circles under her eyes, hair a disheveled mess, skin so pasty white she wouldn't blame someone for thinking she'd recently survived a bout with cancer.

She looked like hell. Felt like it, too.

C.K. Carr

She'd kept her hair long—Dave had always loved her long brown hair—but she should've chopped it off. It just hung there, lank and dry, the victim of too many days when she hadn't had the will to eat or even drag herself out of bed.

She raised an arm that was more bone than flesh and with a deep sigh applied the bright red lipstick she'd always loved.

One glance in the mirror and she knew it would never work. She was too...**withered**...to pull it off.

She'd never been vain about her looks before. Maybe because she'd always known she was attractive, with or without makeup. Now, though...

She tried to scrub the lipstick off with a tissue, but it clung to her skin, red as blood, seeping into the fine lines that radiated outward from her lips.

Thirty-four but she looked fifty.

She almost quit right then. Almost turned away from the mirror and slunk back to the couch where she'd been sleeping since Dave had died. The master bedroom was so full of him, of memories of loving and laughing and building a life together, that she could barely set foot in it.

Tears flowed down her cheeks and she dashed them away.

Damn it. Was it ever going to end? Would she ever move past it?

He'd been gone over a year and she still hadn't made it through a single day without crying.

The unexpected loss of her mother had devastated her, but this…this was a level of pain and emptiness so far beyond that she couldn't even define it.

She was drowning.

Alone, isolated.

Almost all of her so-called friends had long since abandoned her. They'd been there at the funeral, of course, or called or sent cards and flowers. (So damned many flowers.) And her local friends had come around in the month after Dave's death, bringing her food, keeping her company.

But when the months passed and she didn't show any interest in who was getting married or divorced, whose kid was doing what, or who had—heaven forbid—worn a **green** dress to that black and white charity event in San Francisco, they'd faded away, disappearing back into their own lives and leaving her behind.

Truth be told, she preferred it that way.

She hadn't wanted to hear about their little problems and dramas when her husband was **fucking dead**. Did she really care that someone's son hadn't made it into the right **preschool**? No. Because she was **never going to have a child** to send to preschool. They just didn't frickin' get it. Instead of pushing their kids to be perfect they should be hugging them tight and thanking whomever you thank that they had them.

And instead of complaining about how their husbands were too fat or worked too much or spent too much time with the kids instead of them they should be glad they had husbands at all.

She'd kept the words back—barely— but she hadn't managed to hide her contempt.

So they'd left. Slowly drifted away to their own lives while she remained here, stuck in the home she'd shared with him, unable to move forward.

The only ones who still called were Melody and Aidan. But they were halfway around the world and madly in love, glowing from the joy of finally being with the right person.

It hurt to see them so damned happy each week. She was happy for them and glad someone still cared, but...

It all hurt. So much.

Too much.

Shaking, she forced herself to scrub the lipstick and tears from her face and try again, even though all she really wanted was to curl up on the floor until darkness came.

She gripped the counter. She couldn't keep doing this; going over the same thoughts and sorrows day after day, night after night. Dave wouldn't've wanted that for her. He'd hate seeing her like this.

He'd told her once that all he wanted was to see her happy, even if that wasn't with him. And he'd meant every word of it, too. That was the kind of guy he was. Open and loving to a fault.

Ironically, that had been the moment she'd stopped running and finally admitted how madly in love with him she was. Five years she'd spent loving him and leaving him and he'd never wavered, never given up. But when he'd said that to her—that he'd be happy as long as she was—she'd finally realized he was the only man she'd ever wanted.

And the five years they'd had after that...

She sniffed, fighting another bout of tears. They hadn't been perfect. Who was? But they'd been damned good. Too good for anyone else to match.

She closed her eyes, fingernails digging into her palms.

She had to do this.

It wasn't a betrayal of Dave.

She wasn't trying to forget him. She could never forget him.

But it was time to move on, to find a way to live her life without him.

She took three, deep, calming breaths.

In.

Out.

In.

Out.

In.

Out...

She could do this. She could.

Something Gained

   She stepped back from the counter, squared her shoulders, and met her gaze in the mirror.

   It was time. Time to move forward with her life.

CHAPTER 2

Not only did none of the makeup she'd liked before work with her new cadaver-like appearance; she also had nothing to wear.

Oh, she had a closet full of gorgeous dresses—sleek numbers that used to hug her curves in all the right places and all the right ways—but those didn't work so well now that the curves were gone and all that remained were her hip bones jutting out like knives.

By the time she was done trying every single one on, the bright-pink bed in the guest room was piled high with shimmery, shiny fabric; a cascade of bright colors that spilled onto the floor.

Jackie chose a brilliant blue wrap dress. It didn't look like it was supposed to—the tie hung down way too far—but at least she could force it to fit. Sort of.

Shoes were another problem. At least she hadn't lost weight in her feet—everything fit—but after a year of running around barefoot ninety percent of the time, she couldn't stand more than a minute or two in any of her old go-to four-inch pairs.

She finally settled on a pair of silver ballet flats she'd never really worn before. They made her feel short and dumpy, but at least they were comfortable.

When she was all done—makeup on, dress belted tight, shoes and jewelry to match—she studied herself in the mirror, trying to see herself the way a stranger would.

The way a strange **man** would.

She might hate the way she looked, but a stranger wouldn't. He'd see a sophisticated woman, her hair pulled back in a chignon, just the slightest hint of pink lip gloss on her lips, and an expensive dress that hugged her slender frame. Without the old her to compare to, he wouldn't know how broken she was. Not unless she told him.

C.K. Carr

And she'd be damned if she was going to do that. She wasn't looking for a therapist. She just wanted someone to jolt her out of the nothingness she was trapped in.

Her hand trembled as she reached for her clutch.

She wasn't really ready to do this.

But she never would be.

She had to force herself to move forward or else she'd be stuck in this cold, empty house forever.

She took a moment, breathing slowly, blanking her mind, pushing away the horror she felt at the thought of any man other than Dave touching her or looking at her the way he had.

She'd never been like that when she was younger—never been one of those women who fixated on one man and couldn't enjoy the company of another—but Dave had changed her with his love and tenderness and steadfast faith. He was a man unlike any other. And he'd been the perfect man for her.

She could never replace him.

Never.

But she couldn't go on this way. Not for another fifty years....

She shuddered, imaging fifty years of darkness and pain.

She wouldn't make it that long. Not if she couldn't get past this.

She grabbed the clutch. She had to do this.

She had to.

If she couldn't…

She shoved the thought aside and opened the door. A late fall breeze chilled her to the bone as she stepped outside.

CHAPTER 3

Jackie sat in her car outside the bar, shivering as she watched the steady flow of people enter and exit. She didn't recognize a single person. And she didn't want to.

Thankfully, Tahoe was a tourist town, full of a constant flow of new faces who'd be gone in a few days.

Oh sure, there were places the locals went and she knew plenty of folks who came back year after year, but it also had places like this. Places that only out-of-towners went to—where drinks were cheap and company was free, fun, and fleeting.

It was the perfect place to find what she needed.

Because the last thing she wanted was to fall in love again. She couldn't replace Dave and she wasn't going to try. She just wanted to do something, anything to break free from the black hole she'd been living in.

Melody and Aidan had tried to help. They called every week whether she wanted them to or not, and sent her listings for things all the time. Movies she might like, cultural events in the city, ski events in town.

Melody also kept encouraging her to take on new interior design clients even though the thought of decorating someone's home filled her with horror.

They'd tried everything they could think of, but Jackie just couldn't bring herself to do any of it. She'd either spend the whole time wishing Dave was there and wondering what he'd think of it or be miserable because she was surrounded by happy people. And the type of design work she'd done before—with bright colors and wide open spaces—didn't exactly fit her current mood. If she had to decorate a beachfront retreat right now she'd fill it with the dark grays of a stormy sky.

They'd tried—because they were good friends and cared about her—but at the end of the day she had to want to move forward or nothing would help.

C.K. Carr

She'd finally decided this was the only way—a fun, carefree fling with a man who'd remind her she was still alive and that sex didn't always have to be about a soul-deep connection with someone you wanted to spend forever with.

She jerked the keys out of the ignition and shoved them in her purse. She'd decided to do this; she wasn't going to back out now. She pushed the car door open, fighting a gust of wind that pressed her dress against her body and whipped her hair around her face. Shivering, she wrapped her arms close to her chest and moved towards the warmth of the bar and the chance at a new start.

CHAPTER 4

Jackie almost left as soon as she stepped inside. The place was packed with people pressed too close to one another—smiling, drinking, laughing.

Living.

After almost a year alone, the sheer number of people almost overwhelmed her. Add to that the smells of beer and fried food and damp clothes and it was an assault on her senses.

But she fought her way forward, struggling not to snarl at the sight of so much carefree enjoyment, and squeezed into a spot at the bar next to a good-looking man and his two friends who were more focused on the hockey game on the television than one another.

C.K. Carr

The man smiled as she brushed against him and moved over enough for her to lean against the bar. He had kind brown eyes and an Oxford shirt with the top two buttons undone.

She forced herself to smile back before signaling for the bartender. She'd barely had anything to drink since Dave died—too scared that she'd spiral so deep she couldn't get back out—but right now she needed something to take the edge off.

And give her a little liquid courage.

When the bartender finally made it to her, she ordered a whiskey, straight up, and downed it before the bartender could ask if she was going to open a tab or pay cash.

It burned its way down her throat and into her belly, chasing the chill away.

"Another, please." She handed over her credit card.

The bartender raised an eyebrow, but poured another like the consummate professional he was.

"Thanks. Keep 'em coming." She took a slow sip of the second one, forcing herself to savor its smooth finish. She'd managed to resist the temptation of alcohol so far. No point in ruining it now.

The man leaned in. "A whiskey woman in a blue dress. That has the makings of a song."

Jackie willed herself to laugh, focusing on this moment with this man and pushing away the memories of a perfect night spent dancing to jazz music with Dave at a dive bar in Dubrovnik. "Probably a couple jazz songs along those lines, I'd imagine."

"Do you like jazz? I do. Dizzy Gillespie is my favorite." The man leaned closer, casually confident as he took a swig of his beer, his eyes never leaving hers.

"As a matter of fact, I do…" She leaned in and smiled up at him, the old give and take coming back to her as they chatted about jazz and music and dancing.

He was perfect. Just what she needed.

An hour later she'd learned that his name was Jim and he was in town from Ohio with two of his college buddies. He loved to ski and had even skied for his college ski team at Dartmouth, he worked as a manager of a manufacturing plant that made dog food, and had two sisters, both married, a brother who was still single, and three nephews, all under the age of five.

"No kids for me, though," he said, his arm resting casually across the back of the bar stool he'd managed to snag her. "Never been married either. Never met the right woman." He flashed a smile that had probably broken a few hearts over the years. "What about you? Ten kids at home that you left with the sitter for the night?"

"No. No kids." She took a quick swig of whiskey to push back the wave of sorrow that thought triggered.

"Ever been married?" He raised an eyebrow, clearly expecting her to say no.

She knew she should lie. What did the truth matter? She was never going to see him again.

But she couldn't. Even for the sake of moving on, she couldn't pretend she hadn't spent those years with Dave.

As the silence between them dragged out, she took a long swig of whiskey.

Jim pulled back slightly. "Don't tell me you're currently married? Because I'm not that kind of guy, you know. I don't need to play the role of some character in a Kenny Rogers song."

She frowned at him. What was he talking about?

"You know, **Lucille**? Leaves her husband and meets some guy at the bar and then the husband comes in talking about all the kids and the farm she left behind and how he can't do it without her and then she goes to a hotel with the guy she met at the bar but he keeps thinking about the husband instead and how she'd left her husband broken and alone to tend to everything and they're both unhappy and miserable and nothing actually happens between them because of it?"

She shrugged. Didn't ring any bells.

"So?" he asked. "Are you married?"

"No. Widowed." She bit her lip as tears filled her eyes. Damn it. She didn't want to cry, **again**, but it was the first time she'd used that word.

Widow. She was a widow.

"Are you okay?" He leaned closer, concern etched into every line of his face. "When did he die? Last week or something?"

She closed her eyes. What the hell was she doing here?

"Jackie?"

She shook her head, forcing back the tears and meeting his eyes. "No. It was about a year ago."

He relaxed slightly.

White hot rage filled her. Obviously he'd never loved anyone in his life. Not the way she had. Or he'd know that one year wasn't enough.

A lifetime wasn't enough.

"What happened? You're so young." He reached for her hand, brown eyes overflowing with sympathy, voice soft and comforting.

She jerked away from him. "Heart attack."

"Were you there?"

"No." She waved to the bartender and signaled for the check.

She needed to leave.

Now.

She downed the last of her whiskey and slammed the glass onto the counter.

Jim touched her arm, looking confused. "Are you leaving? Don't go."

She ignored him as she signed the receipt—leaving a generous tip—and reached for her coat.

20

"Jackie? Are you okay?"

She shook him off. "I'm fine. I'm sorry. I thought I could do this, but I'm just not ready yet."

She pushed her way through the crowd, struggling to breathe amongst so many people, never looking back, praying that he'd stay where he was and just let her leave.

She should've lied. Given a fake name and a fake story. Or dragged him out of the bar half an hour ago with a coy smile before the conversation could move past who the best jazz musician was.

Tears filled her eyes as she stumbled outside into the chill, dark night, but she refused to let them fall. Not here, not now.

She made her way to her car.

Alone.

Still.

Always.

CHAPTER 5

Jackie didn't even bother changing when she got home, just stumbled to the couch, wrapped herself in the oversized blanket Dave had bought her two Christmases before, and huddled there weeping until exhaustion finally overtook her.

She would've stayed like that the entire next day, but it was Sunday, the day when Melody and Aidan always called. Precisely at ten. No way to claim she didn't know they were going to call and had just missed them.

And Aidan being Aidan, if she didn't answer he'd probably be on the next flight to the States to check on her in person. Or, worse, he'd call the cops and one of Dave's old fishing buddies would swing by to make sure she was alright.

So when the alarm on her phone chimed 9:45, she dragged herself to the kitchen table and booted up her laptop, wishing they didn't insist on video chats each time.

She knew why they did it. They wanted to **see** how she was. Even though she was careful to keep the area directly behind her immaculately clean, it was clear the overall answer was "not good." Two weeks ago, Melody had sent her a chocolate decadence cheesecake that could easily feed twelve. Last week, she'd sent two pounds of fudge and a large tin of caramel corn.

Jackie hadn't eaten any of it—the thought of food turned her stomach most days—but she knew she'd have to start eating something soon or Melody would keep sending impossibly fattening things until she found something Jackie would actually eat.

Jackie wrapped herself in the blanket and curled up on the chair as she waited for Skype to finish one of its eight million unwanted updates that always seemed to happen at exactly the wrong moment.

To think she'd once lived on her laptop. Between work and keeping up with friends who were scattered all over the world, she'd probably spent a good ten hours a day on it. Now the only times she logged on were for these calls. She hadn't been on Facebook since Dave died. Hadn't checked email in months.

Didn't honestly care if she was missing something important either. She just couldn't do it. Not now. Maybe not ever.

She made a little swirly shape in the dust on the table as she waited.

Someone should really clean the place up.

Too bad she was the only one around to do it.

Right at ten, prompt as always, her computer flashed with an incoming video call.

Jackie sighed before forcing a smile and answering. Melody's face appeared immediately. She looked healthy and happy and disgustingly in love like she had every week for the last year. "Hey there!" she called.

"Hey. Where's Aidan?"

"Oh, he's on an overnight charter, so it's just me today. Sorry."

"That's fine." Jackie snuggled into the blanket. "You know you could've skipped it. You don't have to call every week."

Melody laughed. "Of course I do. Someone needs to look out for you, you know." She frowned into the screen, her attention focused somewhere below the camera, probably where Jackie's image was on her computer screen. "Not that we've been doing that great of a job. Did you get the fudge? And the caramel corn?"

"Yes."

"Did you eat them?"

Jackie shrugged. "Not yet. But I promise I'll eat some of it this afternoon, okay?"

Melody pressed her lips together, but nodded. "Okay. You know, what you really need is to be subjected to some of Aidan's cooking. I swear, I've gained ten pounds in the last year."

"He is a good cook, that's for sure. Although I'll never get over the sight of a six-three Irish bloke flipping pancakes while he debates the merits of milk versus buttermilk."

Jackie had known Aidan since she was a kid stuck in Ireland for the summer. That was where she'd met him and Dave. Little had she known then how important they'd become to her.

"I know. It is a sight to see." Melody laughed. "Well, at least with him gone today that gives us a little girl time, right?"

"Right." Although, what did they have to talk about? Melody was madly in love and Jackie was slowly drowning in despair.

Jackie chewed on her thumbnail—a nervous habit she'd never managed to break. Before Melody could ask what she'd been up to for the last week, Jackie asked, "Still enjoying Brazil?"

"Yes...But..."

"But?"

"Well...We've had an interesting offer." Melody leaned forward. "Actually, it involves you. Or it could."

"Involves me? How?" Jackie crossed her arms, not trusting this one bit.

The blanket fell off her shoulders and she tugged it back into place. Melody tilted her head to the side, frowning at the screen, and then sat back with a big smile on her face. "Jackie? Is there something you want to tell me?"

"What are you talking about?" Jackie frowned at the screen.

"Well, let's see…There's the slightly smeared mascara, which I don't think I've seen you wear in a year. And, if I'm not mistaken, that blanket is covering a dress that's not exactly what one wears at ten in the morning on a Sunday. Which means…You were out? And didn't get a chance to change before our call?"

Melody looked so damned hopeful it almost made Jackie start crying again. She pressed her lips together and stared at the wood beams of the ceiling two stories above, fighting to control herself.

"Jackie? Are you okay? Did I say something wrong? I'm so sorry. I didn't mean to. What is it?"

Jackie expelled a deep breath. "No, you didn't say anything wrong. And I am wearing what I wore last night. But…" She couldn't hide the quaver from her voice. "It's not what you think. I wish it were…" Her voice broke and she buried her face in her hands.

"Oh, Jackie!" If Melody could've leapt through the computer, she probably would've. "What's wrong? Please. Tell me."

Jackie wiped the tears from her cheeks. "Nothing. I'm just pathetic and hopeless and...How the hell did I get like this?"

"Of all the women I know you are the least pathetic and hopeless one I've ever met."

"Maybe before." She sank further into the blanket, her shoulders hunched around her ears. "But now...Oh, you should've seen what a disaster it was..."

She told Melody all about it. How hard it was to get ready, how nervous she'd been driving to the bar, meeting Tom and how they'd flirted for an hour... and then his stupid question about whether she'd ever been married and how she'd fled so fast she'd made his head spin.

She sighed as she stared at the computer screen. "I'm never going to get past this, am I?"

Melody chewed on her lip for a moment before answering. "I don't know, Jackie, I really don't." She ran her fingers through her hair with a grimace. "I've learned to live with the loss of my mom, but I've never moved past it. I'm not who I was before. Losing someone like that isn't something you get over, you know? I mean, you lost your mom, too. You get it."

She stared off into the distance as she continued. "And Dave...I mean, my mom was central to my life, but she wasn't my life. But Dave was for you. He was the one you were going to spend forever with. You **shouldn't** just get past losing him. Not when he was that important to you. And especially not for some middle manager from Ohio."

Jackie laughed slightly as she wiped the tears away with the back of her hand. "He did have nice eyes. And I wasn't planning on marrying him or anything. I just thought..." She shrugged. "You know."

"I know. Personally, I've never been able to do that. Before I met Aidan I'd wallow for weeks or months on guys I **knew** weren't worth it. I admire people who can just bounce back and move on to someone new like that."

"It's certainly more fun than wallowing if you can manage it." She smiled weakly, remembering some of her rebound relationships from before she'd married Dave.

"I'm sure. Well, you can always try again, right? That's the good thing about a tourist town? There'll be someone new at that bar next week."

"True..." Jackie picked at the edge of the blanket, unraveling a loose thread loop by loop.

"Or..." Melody leaned forward, a big grin on her face.

Jackie frowned, not trusting that look. "Or?"

"You can come with us to New Zealand! That's what the opportunity is. We're going for the summer season to help Aidan's friend George run a couple of boats in the Coromandel. It's supposed to be gorgeous. You can bring your camera. And we'll go hiking every day and explore the whole area and Aidan can cook yummy meals for us every night. It'll be perfect. Aidan says you already know George and that you guys get along."

Jackie froze. "Are you talking GQ George? About six-three, jet black hair, green eyes, looks a bit like a Greek statue come to life?"

"Yeah, I think that's him."

"No. I can't." Jackie fought the urge to slam the laptop closed. Running off to some tropical paradise to spend time frolicking with her closest friends felt like the worst kind of betrayal of Dave's memory. Add to that the presence of a gorgeous, single man...

No.

Not like anything had ever happened between her and George, but they'd come close a few times and she just couldn't do that. Not. No.

Melody glared at her from the computer. "Calm down. We're not trying to set you up or anything, I promise. Actually...I can pretty much guarantee George isn't going to bother you like that. He's..." She winced. "He's got his own thing he's dealing with right now."

Melody continued, "You'll just be somewhere with your good friends to keep you company instead of trapped in that big, dark house all by yourself. Plus it'll give Aidan a chance to fatten you up a bit which you desperately need. Aidan told me to tell you Dave would want this if he were here."

"That's playing dirty."

"That's Aidan for you." She shrugged. "Plus...I think George could use someone like you around right now. Someone who understands a bit of what he's going through."

"Why? What happened?" Jackie pulled the blanket closer as she leaned forward.

"He, um." Melody winced. "He was in a pretty serious car accident about nine months ago. It's why he needs us to help him out for the summer—he can't quite manage on his own just yet. And, uh, his fiancée was killed in the crash."

"What? How did I not know about that?"

"Well...you've kind of been dealing with your own shit for the last year, you know? And we certainly weren't going to mention it to you what with all you were dealing with already."

Jackie sat back, stunned. She'd been so wrapped up in her own pain and loss that it hadn't even occurred to her that others might be going through a rough time, too. "So how is he?"

"Hard to tell. He's a fairly gregarious guy, so each time he's on Skype with Aidan he's all smiles, but Aidan thinks he's hurting pretty bad. Said it's not like George to ask anyone for help, ever, so the fact that he reached out to us is a pretty big deal."

Jackie nodded as she chewed on her thumbnail. "True. He always was one to do it on his own if he could. Then again, he was always perfectly capable of doing it on his own, too."

"Hm. Sounds like someone else I know." Melody grinned at her.

"Who? Aidan?"

"And you. And probably me. But we all hit our wall at some point, right?" She stared into the computer screen once more. "Breast cancer taught **me** that. Thankfully you and Aidan were there for me when I needed you. So let me be there for you now. Let **us** be there. Come to New Zealand."

"I don't know…" Jackie looked away from Melody's hopeful face. "I'm not sure I feel up to going halfway around the world. And this is my home. I can't just leave it behind."

"What do you have going on there that you can't walk away from?"

"Well, there's my business…"

Melody rolled her eyes. "You haven't taken on a new client since Dave died and I'm pretty sure you're not actively working on anything for any of your existing clients either."

Jackie chewed on the inside of her lip. "It's almost ski season."

"Were you planning on skiing this year?"

"No. But..."

Melody glared her down.

"And someone needs to be here to look after the place." She glanced at the swirly mark she'd made in the dust on the table and winced.

"Ha! Now I know you're just looking for excuses."

"What are you talking about? It's true."

"Hire one of those rental services. They'll clean it up, rent it out, and make you a frickin' fortune over the next few months. How many can sleep there, do you think? Ten? Twelve? Fifty?"

"Not fifty."

"Okay, fine. Not fifty. But plenty. Which means all those college groups that go to Tahoe for a fun weekend would love to rent your place. And that means you have no excuse not to come to New Zealand with us. Plus it's going to be summer in New Zealand. Do you really want to spend another cold, lonely winter there when you can spend a beautiful summer with friends instead?"

Jackie sighed. She didn't really want to spend the winter alone, but...

Melody nodded to herself. "Good. It's settled. Pack your bags, missy, you're going to New Zealand. I'll be there on Thursday to pick you up."

"Thursday? What? I can't possibly be ready by then."

"Too bad, because that's when we're leaving. Pack before I get there or come with the clothes on your back." Melody winked and ended the call.

Jackie stared at the computer screen, her mouth half-open. What had just happened?

She thought about calling Melody back and saying she couldn't do it. But the swirly mark in the dust caught her eye.

She glanced around at the cobwebs in the rafters and the piles of dirty dishes in the sink, and thought about all the empty, dark nights stretching out before her. How much longer could she do this before she just gave up on living altogether?

Not long.

And as much as she would've liked a night with Jim or some guy like him to solve all her problems, she knew deep down that meaningless sex with some nice but boring man wasn't going to fix things this time around.

Which meant...

She was going to New Zealand.

CHAPTER 6

The next Thursday, Melody was true to her word. She pounded on the door and shouted for Jackie to answer, threatening to bust in the window if she didn't do it soon.

Jackie rushed to open the door, knowing that Melody probably wasn't kidding. As soon as she opened it wide enough, Melody burst through, all smiles and talking a mile a minute.

"Hey, there! So good to see you." She hugged Jackie quickly before stepping around her to examine the dark, dusty entryway. "You look like hell, by the way. Did you really not eat the cheesecake I sent? I thought you liked chocolate?"

Before Jackie could answer, Melody had proceeded to the living area where she turned on every single light and then walked around making tsking sounds as she picked up a dirty plate here, folded a blanket there, and generally tidied up more than Jackie had in a year.

Jackie watched from the entryway, arms wrapped tight against her body, absent-mindedly chewing on her thumbnail, feeling equal amounts ashamed and exhausted.

Finally, Melody ground to a halt and turned to face her. "I'm sorry."

The concern in Melody's voice almost undid her, but Jackie clenched her arms tighter and kept her chin up. "For what?"

"For not realizing how bad it was." She leaned against the couch. "For not being here for you."

Jackie shrugged one shoulder. "You guys called every week, what more could I ask for? Plus, the last thing I wanted was to have front-row tickets to your happiness."

Melody winced. "Oh, Jackie...I'm so sorry. I didn't even think..."

"Stop saying you're sorry. There's nothing to be sorry for." She pushed past Melody and grabbed the small duffel she'd packed. "Now, when does our flight leave because I'm ready to go."

Melody looked like she wanted to argue, but didn't. "Tonight. Ten-thirty. Out of San Fran. Is that all you're bringing?"

Jackie nodded.

"Are you sure? What's in there?"

"My camera. My tablet. A toothbrush. Toothpaste. Hairbrush. Deodorant." She'd had to run to the store for the last few items. She'd be damned if she was going to bring the plated-silver hairbrush Dave had given her as a wedding gift and she hadn't exactly been focused on brushing her teeth and putting on deodorant in recent months.

"What about clothes?"

"I have a few sundresses to get me started, but I figured we could pick up new clothes once we're there." She glanced at Melody and away again. "Most of my clothes don't exactly fit these days."

"Oh. Right. I hadn't thought about that." Melody paced the room. "What about…Your phone? Your phone charger? Power cord for the tablet? Anything you need for the camera?

Makeup? Shoes? Your shoes still fit, right?"

"I packed some flip-flops in addition to the tennies I have on. And I'll get some new hiking boots when I get there."

Melody's gaze flickered towards the almost-new pair of hiking boots by the door.

Jackie shook her head. "Too many memories. Dave and I bought those before we went to Yellowstone two years ago."

"Oh. Okay then."

After a long, awkward silence, Melody added, "Then I guess we can get going. Gives us some time to grab a meal on the road since as far as I can tell you don't have a whole lot to eat here." She grinned. "Unless you want a lunch of fudge, caramel corn, and chocolate cheesecake? Because I could be down for that."

Jackie smiled. "No. Real food in a restaurant would be...nice."

"Okay. Then, let's go. New Zealand awaits."

Jackie hesitated.

She didn't want to leave. It felt like a betrayal somehow even though she knew Dave would want her to go and enjoy herself.

Melody squeezed her arm. "You'll be back. It's just a couple months."

"Will I?"

She'd grown up in this place— spending summers and winter weekends at the "cabin" with her family. And then when they got married, she and Dave had made it their home. But something in her gut told her that her time here was over, that once she walked out that door some cord that had kept her tethered to this place would snap and she'd just wander the world, lost and alone, until the end.

"You will. I promise." Melody met her eyes. "And it'll be better when you come back. If Aidan can't set you to rights, I don't know who can." Melody threw an arm around her shoulder. "Come on. Let's get started on our grand adventure."

Jackie let Melody lead her to the door, but she pulled away on the threshold and turned back, certain she was forgetting something.

"You okay?"

Jackie nodded. "I am...I just..." She glanced at the photos hanging on the wall—photos she'd taken during all her and Dave's many travels around the world. Photos from Ibiza and Egypt and Australia and Thailand and all sorts of other fun, exotic places. And there, in the center, a black and white photo of them out on the lake on his boat, the mountains in the background, laughing as they leaned in to take the shot.

Melody nudged her. "You should bring it."

"I..."

Before Jackie could object, Melody lifted the photo off the wall and handed it to her. It was small enough to carry—just a 5x7 frame—but Jackie hesitated. How could she possibly move forward if she was still clinging to what she'd had with Dave?

Then again, it was just one photo.

"Bring it. If you're not ready to have it in your room, I'll keep it for you until you are."

"Okay." Jackie placed it on top of the clothes in her duffle. Her hand rested against the glass for a long moment, as she wondered if she'd ever experience a moment of pure joy like that ever again.

"Come on." Melody carefully guided her outside and pulled the door shut with a hearty slam.

Jackie shivered as wind whipped across the porch, carrying the chill of winter. Hard to believe that in a few short days it'd probably be snowing here but she'd be in New Zealand with an entire summer stretching out before her.

As they walked towards Melody's car, Jackie reminded herself why this was the right thing to do. She'd help Melody with her photography and spend time with George and Aidan and, if she was lucky, keep so busy she didn't have time to think of Dave, not until she finally reached that day when she was far enough from his death to not be overwhelmed by his absence.

Dave would want this for her. He'd want her to be with Aidan and Melody and George instead of withering away alone. They'd been his friends, too. He'd approve.

But it was hard to leave this place behind. Hard to leave all the memories, to let go and risk starting over.

C.K. Carr

She turned to look at the cabin one last time.

So many years they'd spent here...

Leaving was the right thing to do.

It was.

She had to believe that.

But as she opened the car door and buckled herself into the passenger sheet she could barely breathe past the tightness in her chest.

If it was the right thing to do, why did it feel like she was losing him all over again?

CHAPTER 7

They stopped for a late lunch just north of the airport at a small Chinese restaurant Jackie had always loved. Her mouth watered at the smell of egg rolls and her stomach grumbled in anticipation of the world's best cashew chicken.

Melody heard and laughed as they seated themselves at a corner booth away from the bustle of the kitchen. "Glad to see you still have an appetite."

Jackie wasn't sure what to say to that. Sure, she'd lost some weight. It was only natural wasn't it? That she not feel like eating because everything tasted like ashes or that she sleep so much she missed a meal or two some days?

She could've just as easily gone the opposite direction and binged on chocolate and cheeseburgers.

But no one should expect her to maintain the same healthy weight while dealing with the loss of her husband.

She fiddled with her silverware until the waitress brought them menus and two glasses of water in hard plastic cups. She liked Melody. They'd hit it off the moment they met, bonding over a shared love of travel and photography and the experience of losing their mothers when they were in their teens.

But she just didn't know what to say, not after so many months spent alone, so she focused on the menu like her life depended on it until the waitress came back and asked what they wanted.

She ordered crab cheese wontons, egg rolls, egg drop soup, cashew chicken, and a side of steamed vegetables.

Melody laughed. "Are you planning to eat all of that yourself or are you okay splitting it with me?"

"We can split it. I'm sure I won't eat it all. It just sounded good."

Melody nodded and handed her menu back to the waitress and then settled back into the booth, silent. Jackie didn't know where to look or what to say.

Thankfully, the drive down from Tahoe hadn't been as awkward. Melody had happily chatted the whole way down about her time in Brazil and in Ireland before that and about how her photography website was finally taking off and she really wanted to do a trip through the Amazon rainforest at some point but was a little nervous she'd get bit by something venomous or contract some deadly disease no one had ever heard of and bring it back with her and wipe out the world population.

It was a lot to take in after months of silence, but Jackie appreciated that she hadn't expected any sort of response. But now it seemed was different. Melody took another sip of her water as she patiently waited for Jackie to speak—not staring her down, but clearly waiting on her.

Jackie set the silverware aside and folder her hands together on the table. "So…Tell me what happened to George. I tried to go to his Facebook page after your call, but it was gone."

"Where to start?" She ran her finger through the water beaded on the side of her glass. "Did you know he was engaged?"

"No! He's the last guy I ever thought would get married. I mean, he was never short of admirers—all you have to do is look at him to see why—but he never stayed with one girl long enough for it to stick. He wasn't mean or nasty about it, he just moved on easily. And as far as I could tell the women who captured his attention were all perfectly happy with the time they got with him and perfectly willing to let him go when he was ready to leave."

The waitress brought hot tea and Jackie poured herself a cup, relishing its warmth as she cupped it in her hands.

"Yeah, that's what Aidan said, too. A consummate ladies' man, but leaving behind smiles instead of broken hearts."

Melody added two packs of sugar to her cup of tea and stirred slowly before taking a sip. Jackie winced to think how sweet that must taste, but didn't comment as Melody continued.

"Anyway. I guess this girl—she was a local, part Maori, part Swedish if you can picture that—was something else. She was a tour guide and they met at some industry event or another and boom, that was it. Fell instantly in love and were inseparable pretty much from day one. He proposed three months later."

"Three months?" Jackie laughed, trying to picture GQ George so smitten with a woman that he'd propose after such a short period of time.

Melody nodded. "I know. Crazy, right? Aidan used to show me all of George's sappy posts about her because it was so not him. He'd even post poems about her sometimes."

"Poems? George? Are you sure this is the same guy I used to know?"

"Mmhm. And they all rhymed if you can imagine that. **My lady most fair with long dark hair**..." She took another sip of tea and laughed softly. "It was bad. And sweet. You think Aidan and I are over the top, but George and Nellie were just...beyond. All the photos he posted of the two of them you'd've thought they were attached at the hip."

Jackie tried to picture the man she'd known falling that head over heels in love that fast, but she just couldn't.

Then again, who would've thought she'd fall so madly in love with Dave like she had? (Even if it had taken her five years to actually admit to it.)

She poured herself some more tea. "So what happened?"

"You've been to New Zealand, right?"

"Yeah."

The waitress brought the crab cheese wontons and egg rolls, the deep fried yumminess distracting her from saying anything more for a moment as she grabbed a crab cheese wonton, dipped it in sweet and sour sauce and spicy mustard, and took a bite. She sighed in contentment, relishing the crunchy texture and creamy filling, wondering why she'd spent most of the last year living on rice crackers and water instead of bingeing on all of her favorites.

There was something to be said for eating your feelings.

Melody helped herself to two wontons and an egg roll before continuing. "Well, up in that part of the country— hell, in most of the country—it's just one-lane each way with nothing more than a painted line to separate traffic. And lots of twists and turns, so you really can't see what's coming down the road a lot of places. And, of course, so damned many tourists used to driving on the other side of the road that they sometimes forget themselves and go back to it."

Jackie winced. "Is that what happened? Some guy driving on the wrong side of the road?"

Melody nodded as she took a bite of an egg roll. "Yep. Nellie was driving. Came around a corner and there was this camper van on the wrong side of the road. No time to swerve. Nowhere to go if she did. There was a steep drop off to the left and an embankment to the right. The camper tried to get back into the correct lane, which is probably what saved George's life, but it meant they hit Nellie head-on. At least she died instantly."

"Oh no." Jackie leaned back, her appetite suddenly gone. She couldn't imagine what it must've been like for George, to see the woman he loved die. It had been bad enough for Jackie to lose Dave, and he'd died halfway around the world. She couldn't imagine how much worse it would've been to be there and be powerless to stop it. "Poor George. That must've devastated him."

"It did. Good news, I guess, is he was so messed up himself, he doesn't remember anything more than their headlights coming at him."

"So he was hurt, too? You said something about him needing help with things, but..."

The waitress brought their soup, but Jackie pushed it aside. She'd already had enough to eat.

Melody glared her down until she pulled it closer and took a sip. It **was** good—nice and salty and warm. She took another sip as Melody continued.

"Yeah, he was actually hurt really bad. In the hospital for two months, the first couple of weeks in a medically-induced coma because of brain swelling. Also injured his right leg and bruised his spleen. It was a lot to recover from."

"But he has?"

Melody shrugged. "We'll see, I guess. He hasn't said a lot about it, but I get the impression he's still pretty banged up. Won't talk on Skype to Aidan, at least not with the camera on, and said the other day that it was a good thing he didn't care about meeting ladies anymore because they certainly wouldn't want Frankenstein."

Something Gained

Jackie snorted. "He was always a little vain about his looks. I'm sure he looks fine. Probably just some artful little scar to add to his allure."

"You think he was vain?" Melody tilted her head to the side. "The way Aidan described it he never really realized exactly how good-looking he was."

Jackie raised an eyebrow at that one. "Well, he certainly knew the effect he had on women. That was the one thing about him I didn't particularly like—the way he strutted around like he just knew he could have pretty much any girl in the room."

"Except you? Aidan said you guys were never a thing, even just for a night. At least, not that he knew."

"He never tried. Then again, neither did I." She studied the bowl of soup, turning it slowly in her hands. "In a way I guess we were both too much alike. I knew I could have pretty much any guy I wanted and I'm sure he was the same with women. So if I could have anyone there, except maybe him, and he could have anyone there, except maybe me, why put out the extra effort to go for the one person you might not be able to get, especially if you were more interested in fun than anything else?"

She pushed the bowl to the side, ignoring Melody's pointed look. "Plus, Dave and I started up about that time and..." She smiled softly. "Well. When Dave was around I always seemed to gravitate to him. And when he wasn't I always went for someone new who didn't know him. I suspect everyone else saw what was between us long before I did."

"I wish I'd known you guys back then. I bet it would've been interesting to watch."

"You wouldn't've been right there in the mix? There were a lot of cute sailors around, all up for a little fun..."

"No. That's...not me. I would've probably met Aidan, been all smitten, and then pined for him for the next couple of years while perfectly good guys were right there next to me just waiting to be noticed and Aidan was off doing his thing, completely oblivious to my existence. I'm good at wasting my time that way." She blushed and stared at the table, her lips pressed tight together.

Jackie studied her for a long moment. "Do you regret it? Holding out for Aidan the way you did?"

Something Gained

The waitress brought the chicken and vegetables, but neither one reached for it.

"No…" Melody poured herself more tea and dumped another two packs of sugar into the cup. "I mean, what Aidan and I have is incredible. It's everything I thought it had the potential to be and more. I've never been happier in my entire life. All those levels we clicked on before are just made that much better now that we're a couple."

"But?" Jackie leaned forward, surprised and a little concerned.

Melody sighed. "But I wasted **years** on him before we finally got together. I still look back and wish I could've just walked away from him at the start and saved myself all that time tangled up with him emotionally without actually being with him. Sure, it all worked out in the end, but…" She shook her head. "The amount of time I spent hung up on him without getting much of anything back…Who knows what might've happened if I could've just let go and noticed the men around me instead." She stabbed at a piece of broccoli with her fork.

"But you would've never gotten together if you hadn't held out for him."

"I know. But who's to say it wouldn't've worked out fine anyway?" Melody pushed the plate of cashew chicken toward Jackie. "I don't believe there's just one person for each of us. Maybe if I'd let Aidan go I would've met another guy that was just as good for me."

Jackie shook her head and pushed the plate into the center of the table. She was stuffed. And angry. "You can't honestly believe that?"

Melody winced, but she didn't back down. "I do. As great as he is, I don't believe Aidan is the only man who could ever make me happy. I mean, think about that. Billions of people on this planet and there's only **one** out of all of them for me to be with? No. Now, granted, I think the number of men on this planet who could make me as happy as Aidan has is very, very small. Like, ten. But it's not zero."

Jackie raised an eyebrow at that. "Ten?"

"Maybe eleven. What's the current world population?"

They both smiled.

Melody stabbed at her food once more and shoved a carrot into her mouth. "I just can't accept that if Aidan and I hadn't gotten together that that would be it. He's obviously one of the best choices possible for me, and I justified being hung up on him so long because the other men I was meeting just couldn't compare. But I really do think there are other men out there who had the potential to make me just as happy. Or at least happy enough to not notice the difference. Problem is, I didn't meet them because I was so focused on Aidan."

Jackie crossed her arms across her chest, she was trembling she was so furious. "So you think that's my problem? I'm too focused on Dave to get out there and meet someone who'll be just as good for me? That what we had wasn't unique or special. That it can be replaced just like that."

"What? No!" Melody stared at her like a deer caught in the headlights. "I wasn't even thinking about you guys just now." She winced. "Sorry. I should've been, but there I was just babbling on about myself without even considering how it must sound to you."

"Good. Because as far as Dave and I go, you're wrong. What we built together I will never be able to build with someone else. Maybe if I'd never met Dave and had instead met and fallen in love with a different guy what you're saying would make sense. But now that I had those years with him? No. Nothing can ever compare to that."

Melody frowned, but didn't respond. Instead she nudged the plate of chicken towards Jackie. "Are you sure you aren't even going to try the cashew chicken? It's pretty tasty. And you are the one that ordered it. Plus, not like we can take the leftovers with us..."

Sighing, Jackie pulled the plate over and spooned herself up a bit, but she couldn't taste it, she was too upset.

For the rest of the meal they made small talk about the places they'd been in New Zealand on their prior trips, both carefully avoiding any talk of anything remotely serious.

Which was just fine with Jackie because Melody didn't get it.

And why should she? She hadn't lost the love of her life. She couldn't understand the giant, gaping hole that kind of loss left behind and how no one could ever fill it.

Ever.

CHAPTER 8

As they walked through the sliding glass doors at SFO, Jackie winced at the sight of the long check-in line for economy. There had to be at least a hundred people lined up to check-in—a slew of backpackers with a handful of businessmen and families with out of control children scattered throughout.

They had time, but who wanted to wait in a line like that? She'd rather sip wine in a bar somewhere instead.

"You know what…" Jackie dragged Melody to the far end of the Air New Zealand section. The line for first class had a lone man in a suit. She moved to stand behind him. "Come on."

"Jackie…What are you doing? Our tickets are for economy."

"Not for long, they aren't."

"What are you talking about?"

Jackie smiled at her. "It's a long flight. I want to be comfortable. So I'm upgrading. I'm sure they still have room, they usually do."

"Oh, okay. Well, I guess I'll just meet you at the gate then." Melody started to back away.

"What are you talking about? I'm going to upgrade us both."

Melody shook her head. "No. You can't. That's too much. What's a first class ticket even cost?"

The attendant behind the counter signaled them to step forward, but Melody didn't move.

"Come on." Jackie grabbed Melody's arm and pulled her along. "Let me do this."

"But it's so expensive..."

"You were perfectly fine with buying my ticket."

"But that was coach. On sale. And off-season. First class is...a lot more than that."

Jackie yanked the tickets out of Melody's hand and gave them to the agent along with her credit card. "Can you please upgrade us to first class?

And don't tell my friend here what that costs."

As the woman went to work, Jackie turned back to Melody. "That money you spent on my ticket was money you and Aidan worked hard to earn. Whereas this..." She shrugged as she leaned against the ticket counter, realizing that what she'd been about to say was going to come out all wrong. "This is from Dave's life insurance plan. You know he'd want me to put it to this kind of use, right? He was always doing for others whenever he could."

It wasn't. Dave hadn't had a life insurance plan. This was money from the trust her mother had left her. But if it made Melody feel comfortable with the expense, it was a harmless enough lie to tell.

"Are you sure?" Melody glanced towards the long line for economy and then back at the agent.

"Positive. Have you ever tried to sleep in an economy seat on a flight like this? Pure misery."

As Melody continued to hesitate, Jackie squeezed her arm. "Please let me do this? Dave would want it." That part, at least, was true. Dave would've given every last penny he had to help a friend and not batted an eye about it. "And it's the least I can do for you coming to get me and take me to New Zealand for the summer. And for calling every week on top of that."

"But that was just..."

"Please?" Jackie begged.

Melody grimaced, but nodded. "Fine. But meals are on me for the entire summer."

"Deal." Another harmless little white lie.

CHAPTER 9

An hour into the flight, settled into her own personal cocoon of comfort in first class, drinking crisp New Zealand wine, and eating a gourmet meal, Jackie knew she'd made the right choice. She would've been in misery flying in an economy seat, wedged between two men big enough to be linebackers, with the seat in front of her reclined so far she couldn't move without hitting it.

This, on the other hand, was pure bliss. When she was ready to sleep her seat would actually convert into a completely flat bed with a mattress and everything. And for a fourteen-hour flight, that alone was worth every penny.

Plus, this way she didn't have some nosy seatmate asking her what was taking her to New Zealand.

Hopefully Melody would get over letting her pay for it. She knew people were sometimes sensitive about these things even though it never really bothered her. Not unless someone took advantage. Back when Jackie had been traveling with the younger sailing crowd—who were rich in adventures but poor in money—she'd run up against the issue more than once. Early on she'd always tried to pay to upgrade her friends, but she'd quickly found that the people she really liked—the ones who were independent and did for themselves—eventually drifted away, leaving her with the hangers-on whose only interest was how much they could get out of her.

She'd soon learned to hide her money and live like everyone around her. But first class travel was a luxury she'd always indulged when she could get away with it.

She never did convert the seat to a bed. She just watched movie after movie after movie instead. She was too tense, wondering what she'd find in New Zealand. What would it be like to live with Aidan and Melody for the entire summer? She liked them both, but…She hadn't lived with another adult other than Dave in five years. And seeing them together every day, happy and in love was going to hurt.

She didn't want to be that bitter person who hated them for what they had, but she worried she might be.

And what about George? What would he be like now? Would he be the same rock-steady, always smiling man she remembered? Or had losing Nellie changed him? Made him darker and more brooding? Could she handle being around someone who was drowning in the same feelings of loss as she was?

Thinking of the past was no better. The last time she'd flown had been to Malta with Dave. And the last time she'd been in New Zealand had been to tour the South Island with him.

All those memories…

There wasn't a single place in the world she could go and not think of him and what she'd lost. Either it was somewhere they'd been together or she'd be wondering how different it would be with him there by her side to tell his awful jokes and befriend everyone around.

As the plane approached Auckland, she stared out the window at the city with all its water and rolling green hills. It was beautiful.

A small part of her was excited for the adventure to come. After the bleak year she'd had, cooped up at home, barely talking to anyone, the prospect of time spent with her friends almost made her smile.

Almost.

CHAPTER 10

As the plane touched down, Jackie stared out the window, feeling equal measures anticipation and dread.

She'd changed so much. She was no longer the young traveler, her heart soaring with expectation at the prospect of a new country to explore and new friends to meet, knowing that something was bound to go wrong but not caring because it would all be part of the adventure and give her a good story to tell when she returned home.

She knew better than that now. She knew sometimes things went so wrong there w

as no recovering from it. All you could do was pick up what was left and trudge forward as best you could.

She sank back in the seat, squashing her emotions, as they taxied towards the gate.

Melody, who was in the seat across the aisle from her, leaned closer to get a look. "Oh, wow. Isn't it gorgeous? I can't believe we get to be here for the next three months."

Jackie nodded. "Yep. We're very lucky." She slammed the window shade closed.

Melody frowned at her for a moment and then took a sudden, intense interest in whatever show she'd been watching for the last hour or so of the flight.

Jackie sighed.

Great.

The trip had barely started and already she was alienating one of her few remaining friends.

She closed her eyes, fighting against the overwhelming urge to turn around and go home. This whole trip was a giant mistake. Aidan and Melody were probably going to ask her to leave once they saw how horrible she was these days. And then she'd lose them, too, and be completely alone with no one left to turn to and...

She tried to breathe past the tightness in her chest, but she couldn't seem to.

Melody reached across the aisle and squeezed her arm. "It's going to be okay. I promise. You made the right choice coming here."

"I hope so."

"You did."

Jackie leaned back in the seat, fighting against the tears that threatened to overwhelm her. She was not going to start this trip off by crying. She was not.

She closed her eyes and took slow, deep, calming breaths. She could do this. She could.

She raised the window shade and stared at the beautiful blue sky and billowing white clouds, at the water stretching off into the distance, and told herself to relax. That it would be fine. That she was with friends now, that they'd understand how hard this was.

She wasn't alone anymore. She had to remember that.

She wasn't alone anymore.

Slowly, the feeling of tightness in her chest eased and she glanced at Melody,

C.K. Carr

managing a weak smile and nod in
response to Melody's concerned look.

It was going to be okay.

She had to keep telling herself that.
Until maybe, someday soon, she
actually believe it.

CHAPTER 11

They made it through customs and baggage screening in record time. It helped that Jackie had basically no luggage with her and that Melody had left her things with Aidan so she only had a backpack.

Of course, that meant that before Jackie was really ready to, she found herself walking towards the opaque sliding doors that lead to the arrivals hall, the words Kia Ora engraved on them. The doors slid open and she was almost overwhelmed by the crowd of people waiting behind the tensile barrier, smiling eagerly as they waited for their friends and family, talking in a dozen different languages, all looking happy and excited.

Even amongst all those people, Aidan and George were hard to miss. Both were tall—Aidan was a good six-two and George was just a smidge taller than that. And both commanded attention with their slim, muscular builds and classic good looks.

Melody shouted and waved, Jackie trailing along in her wake as she rushed forward to meet Aidan.

Jackie tripped as she came close enough to really see George's face. He was still attractive—the accident hadn't taken away the chiseled jaw, dark hair, and green eyes—but...

But now he also had a jagged ugly red scar running down the right side of his face that cut across his cheek to his nose, pulling his right eye down slightly. He caught her staring and reached to cover it, but then shrugged slightly and lowered his hand again as if to say it was what it was.

As Aidan picked Melody up and spun her around in a circle and then leaned down to kiss her passionately, Jackie made her way to George's side.

"Hey," she said, feeling suddenly awkward.

"Hey. It's good to see you, Jackie." He limped forward, his right leg dragging slightly, and pulled her into a hug, wrapping her in his strong arms and holding her against his firm chest for a long moment.

A shock passed through her at how good it felt to have a man, any man, hold her close. She hadn't been hugged like that since Dave died. Hadn't really let anyone touch her since then. She realized in that moment that it wasn't just Dave she'd lost, but everyone in her life. Every comfort, every pleasure. Like she'd been punishing herself.

She pulled away. Too quickly. "Melody said you'd been in an accident. But..." She tentatively reached up to touch the scar. "I didn't realize you'd been hurt so bad."

"Yeah, doubt anyone'll be calling me GQ George anymore." He smiled, his eyes warm with affection. "You're not looking so great yourself these days, you know?" He stepped back and eyed her critically. "You gotta eat, Jackie. I know it's hard, but you gotta do it."

She couldn't meet his eyes, afraid she'd start crying right there in front of all those people. "Yeah, I know."

He held out his hand. "Here. Let me get your bag."

"It's fine. I can carry it." She gripped the bag tighter and stepped back.

"There's the Jackie I used to know." He laughed. "Miss **I can do it just fine myself, thank you very much**."

"Pot. Kettle." She glared at him, but couldn't keep it up. Even with the scar, his smile was still infectious.

"Good to see you again." He threw an arm around her shoulders. "Glad you're joining us this summer. Not sure I could handle it if I were stuck alone with the two lovebirds." He nodded to where Aidan and Melody were still locked in a passionate embrace.

"Tell me about it. You'd think those two would need air at some point."

"Yeah, guess not. Should we time it, see if they set some sort of world record?"

Aidan finally released Melody. "Jackie! Come here, let me give you a hug," he said in his Irish brogue. He pulled her into a giant bear hug and spun her around in a circle so fast she stumbled when he finally set her back down.

The duffel started to slip from her shoulder but George caught it and slung it over his shoulder with a satisfied smirk. Jackie glared at him for a half second but let him keep it.

George leaned in close. "You've gotta let me feel useful somehow. Especially now. I mean look at me. I'm a limping, scarred mess."

"Oh no you don't. No using your injuries to get my sympathy. I know you, remember?"

"What's that supposed to mean?" George winked at her and nodded towards the exit. "Car's this way. Come on."

As George turned his attention to Melody, Aidan stepped closer. "So? How've you been? How was the flight? Didn't pack much did you?" Aidan prattled on, never once pausing long enough for her to actually answer, as they left the airport and made their way towards the parking lot.

She just listened and smiled. It was good to see him again. He was the older brother she'd never had—a guy with a heart of gold who'd befriended a lonely kid with no friends stuck in a foreign country for the summer. And she'd missed him. More than she'd realized.

Melody poked him in the side. "Aidan, give her a break, would you? We just landed. And I'm not even sure she slept on the flight."

"Ah, come on now. Jackie's like family, and I just want to know how's she's doing." He leaned closer. "I'd say you've lost a bit of weight since I saw you last."

She shrugged. "It's been a hard year."

He squeezed her close. "Well, we'll get you fixed up in no time, don't you worry. A few weeks of my cooking and you'll be all set."

"Aidan, really...I'm fine. I don't need..."

He mock-frowned at her. "Is it my cooking? Have you been lying to me all these years? Telling me you like it when you really think it's absolute rubbish? Is that it?"

"No." She laughed. She couldn't help herself. Aidan was like a bull in a china closet sometimes, but that was what she loved about him. "Just...Just give me a day to settle in and get my bearings before you start trying to force feed me, would ya?"

"Well..." He winced. "It might be a little late for that." He and George exchanged a look.

"What? What did you do?" She pulled away from Aidan and looked back and forth between them.

George shrugged. "We might've arranged a small party at the house tonight so you can meet everyone in the neighborhood."

"We just landed."

Aidan grinned. "Exactly."

"What's that supposed to mean?" She glared at him.

"It means you're too tired to put up a fight and tell us you aren't up to any company and just want to sleep and recover for a few days." He winked at her as he led the way to a Jeep-like vehicle that was so splattered with mud she couldn't tell its color.

"But I **am** tired and I **do** want to sleep and recover for a few days. And I really am not up to meeting strangers right now, Aidan."

Aidan opened the back door and waited until she was seated and buckled in before he answered. "Jackie, you forget how well I know you. If we hadn't had something planned for tonight you would've found an excuse to not do anything or see anyone for the rest of the summer. And **that** simply isn't happening."

She glared at him. "Aidan, I didn't come here to be bullied around by you."

"No, you didn't. But that's what you're gonna get until you stop looking like some combination of a scarecrow and a zombie."

As her mouth dropped open in outrage he slammed the door shut.

George slid into the seat next to her and leaned close, speaking softly as Melody and Aidan got into the front seats. "I know he's annoying as all get out sometimes, but I think he'll be good for both of us. Hard to wallow with someone like Aidan around." There was a look of such supreme loss in his eyes that it made her shiver with understanding.

She nodded. "Yeah, I guess you're right."

As he turned to stare out the window, she studied him. He'd changed. A lot. He still seemed like the same man he'd always been—gregarious, friendly, steady—but there was a heaviness to him now. A shadow lurking in the corner of his eyes that you'd only see if you really knew him well.

She wondered if he saw the same changes in her...

Probably.

She settled back in her seat. As horrible as it was to think it, she was sort of glad she wasn't alone in her grief. Aidan and Melody weren't strangers to loss either, but what she was going through, what George was going through, it was different. Different from any other type of loss.

She hadn't just lost the man she'd loved, she'd lost the dream of the life they'd have. Her entire future. George had, too. He could understand.

CHAPTER 12

The three-hour drive to Whitianga was heart-stopping on more than one occasion. An hour into it, Jackie was wondering if she was going to survive her first day in New Zealand or if Aidan was going to kill them all in a fiery crash. You'd think that would be hard to do in a country with low speed limits and only one lane of traffic in each direction most of the time, but Aidan had a bad habit of passing every car he could every chance he got, even when that chance was slim or the line was a double-yellow.

When they finally pulled up in front of the small, blue house where they'd be staying for the summer, Jackie was wrung out.

So was George. He hadn't spoken the whole time and there were grooves in his palms from gripping his seat belt so tight.

She leaned over. "Next time you drive."

He shook his head. "Haven't been able to sit in the front seat of a car since the accident. Too many memories." He got out of the car before she could apologize.

Melody flashed her a smile. "I'd like to say that was Aidan's way of scaring George back into driving, but I'm afraid that's just how he drives. I guess everyone has to have a flaw. Too bad his is one that'll get us all killed one day."

Aidan winked at her. "You still love me, though."

"Always." Melody smiled at him, her face full of adoration.

While Melody and Aidan leaned in for a quick kiss, Jackie got out of the car. She was happy for them, but it was going to be hard to be around that for the next three months.

George moved to stand next to her. "Did I mention how glad I am you're here and I'm not stuck with just them for the whole summer?" He shook his head. "I guess now I know how my friends felt around Nellie and me."

"Yeah, I guess Dave and I were pretty bad at times, too. Never thought a thing about it at the time."

"Oh, yeah. You two were **awful**. It was like you lived in that man's lap." George winked at her and she laughed. "Come on. Let's get you settled in. Did you sleep at all on the flight?"

"Nope. Not a wink."

She trailed along behind him as he led the way to what would be her new home for the next three months, trying to hide how nervous she felt. It was just three months. And she was staying with friends.

So why was she so scared all of a sudden?

CHAPTER 13

The house was smaller than her home back in Tahoe, but it was in a great location—only about a hundred feet from the beach—and with a back porch where someone could sit and listen to the ocean waves lap against the shore.

Actually seeing the ocean wasn't as easy. The back yard was green and lush and bordered with tall trees that screened it from a direct view of the water as well as prying eyes.

George pointed out a handful of kayaks stacked by the side of the house and told her to use them anytime she wanted and then led her inside.

The living area had two large brown couches that had seen better days and a small but adequate television on a plain wooden stand. It was separated from the long narrow kitchen by a breakfast bar with four mismatched stools. The kitchen cabinets had definitely seen better days, but at least everything was tidy and clean. Leave it to two sailors to keep a shipshape home.

"You want a cuppa?" George asked, nodding to the kitchen where a random assortment of plates and glasses were visible, probably left behind by prior tenants over the years.

"No, I'm good. I think I might just take a nap."

"Well, then, allow me to escort you to your room, my lady. Only the finest for guests of Chez George."

The three rooms and one bathroom were all down a long narrow hallway. George's room was the first on the right with Melody and Aidan's across the hall. He led her farther down the hallway to the second door on the right, which was closed.

He paused with his hand on the door knob. "This will be your room. I thought you might like to have access to the porch. And being across the hall gives a little distance from the two lovebirds. Last thing you need at night is to hear **that**."

She nodded agreement as he opened the door for her with a bow and a flourish.

"Like it?" he asked, watching her with a big grin on his face.

The room was lovely. Everything bright and new. The walls freshly-painted white with a border of blue flowers at top and bottom that matched the bedspread and bedside table.

Someone had spent a lot of time on it.

"It's beautiful. Did you do this?"

"Yeah."

She narrowed her eyes at him. "When?"

George rubbed his chin and stared at the floor. He sucked in air through his teeth. "It was supposed to be for Nellie, but..." He shrugged, scuffing the floor with his foot.

"Did she like it?"

"Never got to see it. I was working on it—as a surprise—at the time of the accident." He glanced at her and away again. "Got the idea for the colors from you, actually. That makeover you did in Half Moon Bay a few years back."

"So you finished it after?"

He crossed his arms, leaning against the doorframe and she realized he had yet to step foot in the room. "I needed something to do with my hands. I couldn't just sit around every night thinking." He nodded towards the border of flowers. "I painted each one by hand while I was grounded."

"Really?" She stepped into the room and studied the first flower above the door. The level of detail up close was stunning. "Wow. That must've taken..."

"Days." He shrugged. "I couldn't sail, so why not? I worked on the bottom row before I could stand for any length of time and then finished with the top row once I was better."

"Well, you did a nice job of it." She leaned against the doorframe opposite him. "And I have to say your method of coping was a helluva lot better than mine."

"Why? What'd you do?"

She blushed. "Sat around in my pajamas, crying, most days. When I bothered to get up, that is."

He grinned, the scar pulling at his eye. "That's what I **wanted** to do. But I knew Nellie'd come back and kick my ass if I tried. It was tempting anyway, just to see her again...But..."

He shook his head. "Anyway. I'll leave you to get settled in. Bathroom's across the hall. Spare towels are on the top shelf in the closet. Only a handful of hangers, but doesn't look like you'll need much more than that." He handed her the duffle, still not stepping into the room.

"Thanks." She watched him walk down the hall, limping slightly.

He stopped and turned back to her. "I really am glad you're here, Jackie. It's good to have an old friend around."

"Yeah, me too."

She stepped into the room, closed the door, and leaned her forehead against it, overcome with emotion. It was good to be here with friends and surrounded by beauty. But seeing George's pain reminded her of her own and of everything she'd lost when she lost Dave.

It was hard.

She turned to study the room—a room decorated by a man deeply in love, every inch of it perfect. She walked around the space, studying each of the flowers—all hand-painted and unique. This is what he'd done **after** Nellie was gone. His shrine to her. And now Jackie was staying in it.

Ruining its pristine purity.

She touched the white teddy bear sitting on the bedside table, the small tag on its ear scrawled with, "To Nellie, Love Always, George". Hard to image the GQ George she'd known writing that. But he had.

He'd changed. In a good way.

She pulled the picture of her and Dave sailing from her duffel and set it on the table next to the bear.

Without Dave she felt unmoored, adrift, not sure what to think or feel or want. But the picture anchored her, reminding her that she'd once been fortunate enough to have the love of an amazing man and that he'd want her to live her life, to enjoy what she had and where she was.

She pressed her fingers to her lips and then to the photo, fighting the urge to cry. She wanted more than anything to see Dave one last time, to have him hold her close and tell her how much he loved her, to kiss him and tell him how much she loved him.

She closed her eyes and took a deep breath.

It was hard to step out of the misery she'd chosen for herself. To let go of what she'd once had and look forward to an uncertain future.

She couldn't do it.

Not yet.

For now it would have to be enough to focus on the moment, to not think too much about the empty road stretching out before her.

She pulled back the clean, crisp sheets and lay down, still dressed, knowing she should probably take a shower after the long flight but not caring enough to get back up.

She curled up under the blue and white comforter and fell asleep to the sound of her friends laughing somewhere nearby.

For the first time in ages she slept peacefully, undisturbed by grief-filled dreams and tears.

CHAPTER 14

By the time Jackie awoke, the party was in full swing. She peeked out the door from her room onto the patio and saw more people than she'd talked to in the last year gathered together out back, laughing and talking in a multitude of accents and at least two languages. (Somewhere nearby a man and a woman were talking German, clearly flirting with one another, even though she couldn't see them.)

She closed the door and lay back down. She'd pretend that she'd been so tired she'd just slept through it. No one could blame her for that, could they? She'd only just arrived in the country after all.

But just as she'd decided that would work, there was a loud knock on the door to the hallway. "Jackie, get up. There's food that needs eating and people that need meeting."

Aidan.

Of course he'd insist she attend. She glared at the door for a long, long moment, trying to decide whether she could safely ignore him. Or, if not that, then cuss him out and make him feel guilty enough to leave her alone.

"If you aren't in the kitchen in ten—I know you'll wanta pretty yourself up—I'm coming in to get you. And don't think locking the door will stop me either. I can take this thing off its hinges in less than five minutes if I want."

Jackie glared daggers at the door, but she rolled out of bed, knowing it was impossible to fight with Aidan when he made his mind up about something.

She took a moment to run a cheap plastic brush through her hair and change into a yellow sundress she'd never worn before—a gift from her sister that had always been too small and now hung from her like an oversized sack—before shuffling reluctantly down the hall.

She didn't even bother stopping by the bathroom to look in the mirror. She didn't honestly care if she looked good or not. She wasn't trying to impress anyone.

George was standing at the end of the hall with two beers in his hands. He thrust one at her as soon as she got close. "Here. It'll help. I promise."

She stared at the bottle, unsure how getting drunk was going to help.

He leaned closer. "You don't have to drink it, just make Aidan and Melody and everyone else think you are. And smile every few minutes so they think you're having a great time. Manage that and they'll leave you alone." He took a swig of his own beer. "I find it's the best way to keep the awkward questions to a minimum. No one wants to ask how you're feeling if it looks like you're actually happy. Come on. I'll show you around."

He led the way towards the kitchen and she trailed along behind him, wanting to run back to her room and lock herself inside. People glanced at her, full of curiosity, but no one approached. They all looked friendly enough, but she felt awkward and out of place.

She'd always liked to socialize, but with smaller groups of people she knew. This was…uncomfortable.

She took a quick sip of the beer. It was nice and refreshing, but hardly tasted like a beer at all. She glanced at the bottle and saw that it was a Monteith's Radler. Well, that made some sense then. It was as much lemonade as beer.

She crept closer to George. He'd stopped at the end of the counter and grabbed a handful of chips. "I'm not sure I can do this," she whispered.

"Don't worry. I'll keep everyone at bay if that's what you need. Want some ham?" He nodded towards where Aidan was busy slicing up an entire pig.

She shook her head violently. "No."

"No worries. Come along. We have other choices." George steered her towards the patio, waving to Aidan as they walked by. Aidan caught her eye and smiled, pleased she was sure that he hadn't had to drag her out of her room.

She stuck her tongue out at him.

George led her to a spot along the far side of the porch where it was mostly dark and, thankfully, quiet. They could still see everyone, but it was just enough out of the way that no one paid them much attention.

"This is better," she sighed.

He nodded his agreement, taking another sip of his beer, as they leaned against the railing in companionable silence.

It was a gorgeous night, just a little bit cool, with a sky that was clear and a moon that was almost full. Behind the sounds of the partygoers, insects chirred somewhere nearby.

"You hungry?" George finally asked.

"Not for pig, I can tell you that."

"Oh, there's some chips and dip and things down there. Want me to grab you a plate?"

"Sure. That's be great. Thanks."

"Anything in particular you want?"

"No. Just whatever."

People called out to George as he made his way down the steps to a large picnic table in the center of the yard. He waved his beer and nodded and smiled, but didn't stop to talk. Most watched him for a moment after he'd passed, but then quickly turned back to their conversations. He was right. If you smiled and had a drink, they did leave you alone.

He brought back one plate full of cheese and carrots and chips and another with a variety of cookies. It wasn't the most well-balanced meal, but at least the smell didn't make her ill.

"Thanks." She took a shortbread cookie from the nearest plate.

"No problem."

He leaned on the railing as she nibbled the food, watching the crowd once more.

It was nice to have someone nearby that didn't demand she interact. Finally, though, she asked, "So, who are all these people?"

He shrugged. "Some are Nellie's family. See that group down there? The man in the blue shirt is her father. And some are local tour guides. A handful that worked with Nellie and others that run boat tours like I do. That couple over there are our neighbors on the north side and that group right there are the current crew staying at the house to the south of us, but half of them'll be gone by month's end."

C.K. Carr

A tall man walked out on the porch, a twelve-pack of beer in hand. He saw George and immediately walked over. "Hey, George, this the new housemate?" He had a funky accent, but she liked it.

He threw an arm around George's shoulder and eyed Jackie with far too much interest. "Didn't tell me she was a looker." He winked at her before someone shouted his name and he turned to wave to them. "Just a minute," he shouted back. "Meeting my future wife here."

George elbowed him in the gut. "Take it easy, Kev. She's had a rough year and doesn't need the likes of you making it worse."

"That's okay." Jackie surprised herself, but added, "No harm done."

It was nice to be around someone who wasn't treating her like a fragile vase that might break at any moment. And his smile was downright infectious.

"Kev." He held his hand out.

She took it. "Jackie. Nice to meet you."

He held her hand for a second longer than he really needed to, staring into her eyes with his intense blue ones.

"Kev, get in here and give me a hand would you?" Aidan shouted from the doorway.

"Yes, sir. Right away, sir." He shrugged his shoulders, backing away without taking his eyes off her. "Until next time." He winked at her and turned to shout at Aidan. "What am I helping with that was worth abandoning my future wife for?"

George shook his head. "Kev's a character, but he's a good guy. I'd trust my own sister with him."

"Oh, I'm sure he is. And he was definitely entertaining, but I'm not ready for anything yet." She winced, remembering that disastrous night at the bar back in Tahoe.

"I know how that feels." George took another long swig of beer and went back to leaning on the railing, staring off into the distance in silence.

It didn't last long. Aidan spied them on his way back inside. "There you are. What do you think, Jackie? Like the place? Like your room?" He nodded at her plate. "Had a chance to try my amazing onion dip, I see."

She snorted. "Your amazing onion dip? Is there some secret to how you make yours that I'm not aware of? Because last time I checked you just dump soup mix in sour cream and stir."

"Ah, yes, see, I stir in a bit of Irish love. Makes all the difference."

Jackie laughed. "You're such a goof."

"I know. But it's why you love me, isn't it?" He kissed her on the cheek. "Best get back inside. I have spinach dip baking in the oven."

He stopped in the doorway to look back at them. "You two be sure to have fun, alright? None of this moping in the corner all night."

"Oh, we will." George held up his beer, a smile plastered on his face. "Promise."

He waited until Aidan disappeared back inside before turning back to her. "Had enough yet?"

"Yes."

"Me, too. But we can't just escape to our rooms or Aidan'll find us and drag us back to the party." He grabbed her hand. "Come on. I'll show you my secret hideaway."

CHAPTER 15

George led her to the far end of the porch where a small two-person swing sat. It was dark there, but not so dark they couldn't see each another. He sat down and patted the cushion next to him. "Here. Sit. It's a little light on the padding, but good enough. And I oiled the hinges so it doesn't squeak too bad."

She sat down next to him, careful not to move the swing.

They could still hear the sounds of the partiers out in the yard, but couldn't see them because the swing was tucked away in a spot where the house dipped inward three or four feet, creating a nice little nook at the end of the porch.

C.K. Carr

"This is my home most nights," George used his leg to move the swing gently back and forth.

"What is?" Jackie stared at him, confused.

"This swing." He took a sip of his beer. It was at least his second if not third. "I don't sleep much. It's...too weird to be in bed and not have Nellie snoring next to me. So most nights I come out here and stare at nothing until I either get so tired I can't stay awake another moment or dawn arrives."

"I know that feeling. I've been sleeping on the couch since Dave died. Can't bring myself to sleep in the bed. Too many memories."

George nodded as he continued to rock the swing. "It's nice out here. You can hear the waves and the bugs and it always smells fresh and clean. The best nights are the ones when it rains and I can sit here all sheltered and safe and watch it come down."

She bit her lip, unsure he'd want to talk about it, but curious. And the space seemed to invite confidences. "When was the accident?"

He paused in rocking the swing for a second, but then kept going. "Nine months ago. January 2nd. Two days after New Year's."

"Melody said you were in the hospital for a while after it happened?"

"Yep. Two months, one week, and four days. Couldn't do much at all for another month after that, but I wanted to get the hell out of that place as soon as I could. Luckily Nellie's family chipped in around here and helped out while I was in and after I got out."

"It looks like you have a good community here. You're lucky."

He laughed softly. "I do. But it also helps that I owe 'em money. Nellie's dad helped me buy this place after I proposed. Pretty sure it was his way to make sure we stayed in New Zealand and I didn't take his baby away. She was his youngest and you know us sailing types." He winked at her before taking another drink. "We tend to wander."

"That you do. Her father was a smart man to lock you down like that."

"That he was."

"You ever think about leaving, now that she's gone?"

He stared off into the distance for a long while before answering.

"Sometimes. But I don't think anywhere else would be any better. And I have the house now and my business and friends who look out for me."

"You owe them money, too?" she teased.

He snorted. "No."

"You're lucky they stuck around. I chased most of mine away in the first few months after Dave died. Couldn't keep up a good face and pretend I cared about what they did anymore."

"Yeah, I guess I'm pretty good at hiding things like that. As far as most folks are concerned I'm still the same old fun-loving, carefree George they've always known. I still tell a good joke and am up for a beer when the sun goes down. They see the scar, but they don't see the rest of it."

"But you're not the same are you?"

She wanted desperately to know that it was normal to feel like she did. To feel like you'd been hollowed out and left with nothing inside.

"No. I'm not. But I learned when my dad died that most folks don't get it. And rather than go through that again, I just let 'em see what they want to see."

Jackie nodded. He was right. Too bad she couldn't hide it the way it seemed he could.

They sat there in quiet companionship until Aidan finally found them and dragged them down to the party.

Jackie tried to protest, but when Aidan set his mind on something it was nigh on impossible to fight him. And she did end up enjoying herself. Kev found her once again and flirted outrageously with her for a good half hour until George finally chased him off with a gentle cuff on the ear. After that she had a lot of nice, harmless conversations with perfectly pleasant people who seemed genuinely nice and happy.

It was good.

That night, as she lay in bed, exhausted, she acknowledged that coming to New Zealand had been the right choice for her. She could socialize, safe in the knowledge that her friends were there for her if she needed it. Friends who understood loss and knew that moving on wasn't some straight line where you just decided to do it and made it happen. That she'd have setbacks here or there.

C.K. Carr

Already, though she'd made it through an entire day without the memory of Dave weighing down her every step. Maybe, if she was lucky, she'd make it through a few more.

And then a few more after that.

She let herself believe that she really could heal and move forward.

As she lay there, she heard a board creak and the soft squeak of the swing as George settled into place for the night, taking up his lonely vigil. Some night she'd go out there and keep him company, help lessen the burden a bit.

Some night, but not tonight.

She turned on her side and stared at the picture of her and Dave, wishing more than anything that he was there to hold her as she finally drifted off to sleep.

CHAPTER 16

The next morning, Jackie awoke to the smells of cooking bacon and coffee. She stumbled blearily towards the delicious scents to find Aidan in the kitchen cooking while Melody sat at the counter reading something on her laptop.

Jackie poured herself a cup of coffee and went to join Melody. "Where's George?"

"He had an early morning charter," Aidan answered. "Left before dawn." He set out three plates and heaped more food onto each one than all three of them could possibly eat in a day. Bacon, eggs, fried potatoes, and French toast.

Jackie stared at him and then back at the plate.

He shrugged. "Wasn't sure what you'd be in the mood for. There's fruit in the fridge, too, but I expect you to eat at least two slices of bacon and some of those potatoes. Need to get some meat back on those bones of yours."

She shook her head as she pulled the plate closer. It smelled delicious, but up close she wasn't sure she could actually eat any of it. She poked at the eggs with her fork. "You aren't helping him with the charter?"

"No, not this one. It was a small group—only three clients—so he told me to hang back and get you started off on the right foot." He set out ketchup and salsa. "I'll go meet up with him around eleven when his second group is scheduled. That one has twelve and we're taking the real boat out."

Under Aidan's expectant gaze, Jackie took a bite of the French toast. It was delicious—the bread was perfectly cooked and sprinkled with powdered sugar and cinnamon and stuffed with a cream cheese and blueberry mixture that was to die for. She sighed in happy contentment.

"You like it?" Aidan grinned at her.

"I **love** it. But no way I'm going to eat all of this in one sitting."

"That's alright. I'll finish off whatever you girls don't manage to eat."

"How can you eat like that and stay so skinny?"

Melody laughed. "Haven't you noticed? He's always on the move. This morning before breakfast he went out kayaking five miles."

"You shoulda come with me."

"Ha. I was happily sleeping, thank you very much. Speaking of…How'd you sleep? Is the room to your liking?"

"Oh, absolutely. It's gorgeous. Have you seen it?"

Melody shook her head, but Aidan nodded. "He put a lot of effort into it." He turned to Melody. "He'd meant it to be for Nellie."

Jackie nodded. "He hand-painted every flower on the wall. It's amazing work. He has a real talent."

They ate in silence for a few minutes, but finally Jackie couldn't resist. She had to ask Aidan what he thought. "So how bad is he really? It's so hard to tell, he does such a good job of hiding it."

Aidan laughed.

"What?"

"Says the woman who was keeping one little part of her place all spiffed up so we wouldn't know how bad she was."

Melody slapped at his hand. "You weren't supposed to mention that."

"What? It's true, isn't it?" He turned to Jackie. "I mean, we saw that you were getting skinny and heard the change in your voice and you not wanting to do anything, but I had no idea how bad off you really were."

Jackie set down her fork and stood up. "Thanks for the food. It was delicious. I think I'll go get settled in now."

"Oh, Jackie, don't let him bother you. You know how Aidan is. Too direct for polite company most of the time." Melody shot him a dirty look. "He's just worried about you is all."

She crossed her arms across her chest, glaring at both of them. "Well I'm here, aren't I? And I went to your party last night, didn't I?"

They both stared her down, but neither one said anything else.

Jackie shook her head and turned to go, but Melody moved to block her.

Something Gained

"Wait. Before you disappear. You, my friend, need clothes. How about a little trip into Whitianga to get some of the basics? You might have to settle for shorts and t-shirts from the local surf shop, but at least we can find you a few things to see you through."

Jackie wanted to say no. She didn't want to go to Whitianga or anywhere else for that matter.

But in her own way Melody was as relentless as Aidan. She wouldn't let it go until they'd gone.

"Fine. Just let me take a shower and then I'll be ready to go. Do you have a hair dryer I can use?"

"No. I've always just let my hair air dry."

"George does. Heard it running this morning." Aidan grinned. "He might be a little banged up, but at least in that respect he's still the same old GQ George we've always known."

Jackie shook her head, smiling slightly.

Aidan pushed her plate at her.

"What?"

"Just a few more bites. I can eat a lot, but I can't eat that much."

"Oh, I'm sure you could if you wanted to."

Aidan just waited, not saying what she knew they were all thinking. That five bites of food wasn't enough. Sighing, Jackie sat back down and picked up her fork.

Melody and Aidan chatted about the party the night before while Jackie forced herself to eat a little more, glad that, if nothing else, it was all delicious

As she swallowed down her coffee and took another bite of eggs, she reminded herself that, as much of a pain as it was to have them hovering over her like this, it was good, too, to know that someone cared.

She wasn't alone anymore.

CHAPTER 17

The pickings in Whitianga were slim. Just a handful of small stores on the town's lone commercial strip, none of them with the types of clothes she'd normally wear.

It didn't matter, though. All she needed was something to cover up her body enough to not scandalize the neighbors. (Although she suspected from her conversations the night before that the neighbors to the north wouldn't bat an eye at her walking around buck naked. Still. Even if they wouldn't mind, she would.)

After checking out all the available choices, she and Melody headed back towards the surf shop. It was almost summer, after all, and if she was going to spend her days hiking, she figured t-

C.K. Carr

shirts, swim suits, and shorts were the perfect choice. Better than the "fashionable" choices in the other stores.

She grabbed a handful of things to try on and ducked behind the dusty fabric curtain of the lone changing room at the back of the shop. The first item she tried on was a sporty little two-piece in a size six, one size smaller than her old size.

The bottoms fell off her hips and the top gaped so bad there was no way she'd be able to wear it in public. Staring at herself in the changing room mirror, one hand holding the top closed, the other holding the bottoms up, she finally admitted that she really had lost too much weight. She'd known she'd lost some and that it probably didn't look good, but this...

Each rib was clearly visible. And her hip bones jutted from her flesh like bad 80's shoulder pads. Even models in fashion magazines weren't this skinny. (And some of those girls looked like they hadn't eaten in the last decade.)

"You have the first one on?" Melody asked. "Let me see."

"Ah, no. A little too big. Give me a sec."

She dug through the clothes she'd grabbed, but they were all too big. The pair of size-four shorts fell off immediately, too. She couldn't even do the low-rider thing with them.

Tears prickling her eyes, Jackie sat down on the rickety little stool, wanting to just give up and go home. Back to her dark little hellhole where no one could see what a mess she was.

"Jackie? How's it going in there? You find anything that fits yet?"

"No. They're all too big." She shoved the handful of suits and shorts through the curtain at Melody.

The storekeeper—a nice older woman with the trace of a German accent—bustled over. "Don't worry. We'll find her something. Let me see what she's tried so far...Oh, okay. Let me see..."

Jackie rested her head against the wall as she waited, wanting to just get dressed and leave but not having the energy to do so.

Finally, the lady came back.

"Jackie? You ready for a few more things to try on?"

"Sure."

Melody handed through a couple swimsuits, three pairs of shorts, and four t-shirts. Jackie stared at the t-shirts for a long moment. One had a comic version of a kiwi across a turquoise background. She checked the tag. "These are kids' clothes."

"I know. But they're pretty much all she has that might fit you. We could go back to that fashion store down the block and see if maybe some of the dresses would work...but not exactly easy to hike in."

"No. It's fine." Jackie threw on the t-shirt.

It fit. A child's size medium and it fit. A bit snug across the chest, but not so snug she couldn't wear it.

She followed that up with a pair of boy's board shorts that also fit. Great, just great.

"Did they work? Can I see?" Melody asked.

Sighing, Jackie pulled aside the curtain.

"Oh, good. They do."

"I look like a twelve-year-old."

"Jackie...with boobs like that, you most definitely do not look like a twelve-year-old. And just because you bought kids' clothes doesn't mean anyone will know it."

Something Gained

Jackie glared at herself in the mirror, arms crossed. Melody was probably right, but that didn't mean she had to like it. "Alright. Fine. Grab me one of every color of each of these." She rolled her eyes. "What other whimsical designs am I going to have to wear? Psychedelic flowers? Kittens?"

Melody grinned at her. "Honestly, it's not that bad. And do you really want one of each? You're going to outgrow these things fast if Aidan has any say in it. We just need to find you a few things to tide you over for the next week or two."

Jackie glanced at herself in the mirror. Melody did have a point...But, still. What harm was there in buying a few extra outfits? Even if they did make her look like she'd stepped out of some guy's demented porno dream...

She glanced at the storekeeper who was standing off to the side trying not to eavesdrop. No one else had come through the entire time they'd been there. How much business did a store like this even get? One, maybe two customers a day?

And not like she couldn't afford it...

"What can I say? I like to wear different outfits every day."

Melody stared her down. "Last week, before you left for New Zealand, what did you wear on Monday?"

Jackie thought back on it. "Monday? My pajamas. I don't think I changed out of them all day."

"Mmhm. And Tuesday?"

Jackie winced. "My pajamas."

"The same ones?"

She nodded.

"And Wednesday?"

"Uh…"

"Exactly. Before you came here you were wearing the same clothes day in and day out and not giving it a second thought. So a few more weeks with a limited wardrobe isn't going to kill you. Okay?"

"Okay. Fine. I'll only get seven tops, five pairs of shorts, and three swimsuits. Happy?" Jackie pulled the curtain closed, ignoring the open-mouthed surprise on Melody's face. She didn't care. Somewhere some little kid was going to be very happy in a few weeks when Jackie donated these ridiculous clothes to the local thrift shop.

Something Gained

And that was okay with Jackie even if it scandalized Melody.

CHAPTER 18

They walked down the main strip to the Tip-Top ice cream shop at the end of the block. Mid-week there was almost no one around. It was still too early in the season for the slew of European backpackers that would pass through over the summer months.

The lad behind the counter tried to talk them into ordering hokey pokey—vanilla ice cream with bits of crystalized honey in it—because that was the quintessential New Zealand flavor and all tourists just had to try it but Jackie insisted on chocolate mint instead. She needed comfort food not a touristy experience.

They sat outside at a little metal café table that leaned dangerously to one side. The matching metal chairs weren't all that comfortable either, but it was a nice day and Jackie enjoyed the feel of the sun on her face and the taste of ice cream on her tongue.

It had been too long since she'd enjoyed either one. She'd had a huge deck at the cabin that she used to sit on all the time in the summer months, but after Dave had died it somehow seemed wrong to go out there and take pleasure in a sunny day when he could no longer take pleasure in anything.

Looking at it now she realized how foolish she'd been to deny herself small pleasures just because he wasn't there to share them.

As she leaned back, eyes closed, enjoying the feel of the sun on her face, she heard a familiar voice say, "Must be my lucky day. My tour is canceled because the bus got a flat tire, I come into town to console myself, and what do I see? The two most beautiful women I know."

She opened her eyes to see Kev standing about two feet away grinning at them.

Melody laughed. "Didn't anyone tell you, flattery will get you everywhere? Pull up a seat."

He looked to Jackie, one eyebrow raised, and she nudged the seat next to her in his direction. "Please."

"Excellent."

For the next thirty minutes, Kev had them in stitches, telling stories of all the crazy tourists he'd met over the years. But he wasn't mean-hearted. Half of his stories involved some foolish thing he'd said or done and how his poor tour guests had been forced to react to his craziness.

Jackie laughed so hard her stomach hurt and tears rolled down her cheeks.

She liked the way Kev's eyes crinkled at the edges and how he was so relaxed with her and Melody, no tension or undercurrent, just a laid back man telling stories.

She was almost sad when his phone rang and he had to leave them to go meet up with the tour bus that had finally fixed its flat tire. But he winked at both of them and swore they'd see him again even if he had to be so rude as to knock down their door someday.

Only as he strolled away, whistling to himself, did she realized that Dave hadn't crossed her mind once while Kev was there. She'd been so busy laughing and talking that she hadn't had time to think about him.

It startled her. How could she do that? Just forget the man she'd loved more than anyone? But then she shook the thought away.

This was good. This was how people moved on and lived lives.

It was a small step in the right direction.

She wasn't going to pretend, though, that this meant the end of her grieving. Oh no. Far from it. But it at least felt like a cracking of the wall she'd built around herself since Dave died. And that was a very good thing indeed.

CHAPTER 19

When Jackie finally pulled her eyes away from Kev she found Melody grinning at her. "What?"

"Nothing. Kev's a nice guy, isn't he? Funny as hell, too."

"Yeah, he is."

"Don't glare at me. I'm just sayin'." But Melody couldn't keep the teasing smile from her face.

"I just got here yesterday! Give me a little time to breathe before you go trying to set me up."

"I wasn't trying to set you up. I was just...commenting...that Kev is a nice guy. And pretty good-looking. And somewhat chill from what I understand. So if you were thinking about trying that whole find someone to help you get back into the dating scene thing, well...You could do worse."

Jackie shook her head. "Great, I'll keep that in mind. So, back to the house now or what?"

"Actually...There's a showing of the new Jason Statham movie at the theater in half an hour if you're interested."

"I thought that wasn't even out yet. Didn't we see a commercial for it at the airport?"

"It's not out in the States yet. Won't be for another month. But it is here. One of the perks of being in New Zealand it seems. And nothing like an action movie to take your mind off things, right?"

"Right..." Jackie tried to hide her skepticism but Melody clearly saw that she wasn't buying it.

"Okay, so maybe not. But can we please go? I love me some Jason Statham."

Jackie laughed. "Should Aidan be worried?"

"Ha! No. Last I checked Statham was with a Victoria's Secret model half his age. No risk he'd look my way." She patted her ample hips. "And not like I'd want him anyway. The effort involved to try to match a man who looks like that? No thanks. So? You in?"

"Sure."

Melody stood and threw her napkin and ice cream cup in the trash. "Come on then. Don't want to be late. Even though we'll probably be the only ones in the whole theater."

Jackie followed along. Not like she had anything else to do. And Melody wasn't about to let her do what she really wanted, which was go home and sulk in her room for the rest of the day.

CHAPTER 20

Thankfully, the movie was entertaining enough to keep Jackie's attention and the type of Jason Statham movie that Melody approved of. She was grinning ear to ear as they left. "I just love when that man plays a rough-exterior-but-heart-of-gold-type role. Mm. So yummy. Especially that scene where he was all shirtless and wet and..."

Jackie laughed. "Well, I'm glad you enjoyed yourself."

"Didn't you? Please tell me you did and it wasn't two hours of agony."

"I did, actually, thank you." She glanced around. "So where to now Miss **I'm Never Going to Give You Time to Think**?"

A little part of her was almost hoping they'd see Kev walking down the street.

She wasn't ready to start anything with him, but she had enjoyed flirting with him.

Melody glanced at her phone. "Probably safe to head back. The boys should be home soon. Unless you want to hang around here?"

They both looked up and down the empty street. At four in the afternoon on a weekday before tourist season, the place wasn't exactly hopping.

"No, I think I'm good." Jackie led the way towards where Melody had parked the car. "You forget, I've spent most of the last year curled up at home on my couch either crying or sleeping."

Melody's car was just across the street. Jackie looked to the left, didn't see anyone coming, and started to cross, but Melody grabbed her arm and pulled her back just as a car whizzed by from the right.

Jackie was about to cuss him out for driving the wrong way when she realized it was actually her fault for forgetting she was in New Zealand. Why people around the world couldn't all drive on the same side of the road she would never know.

"Gotta watch out," Melody said as they both started across the street.

"Yeah. From now on I'll just look in all directions before crossing the street."

"Good idea. Especially with tourist season about to begin. Last time I was here I lost count of the number of times I saw someone driving the wrong way, usually just in a parking lot thankfully. Half the time it was one of those crazy Wicked campers. You know the ones I'm talking about?"

They made their way towards the car. "Mmhm. A guy I was hanging out with and I rented one when I was twenty-three. Drove all over the South Island in it. It was great."

"This was pre-Dave?" Melody unlocked the door for her and moved around to the driver's side.

"No..." Jackie slid into the front seat, blushing slightly. "This was during that five years when I kept meeting up with Dave on my travels, getting overwhelmed by my feelings for him, and running away as fast as I could." She shook her head. "The number of years I wasted running away from that man..."

"Well, maybe you needed them. I figure if Aidan and I had gotten together right away we wouldn't have lasted. We're both too guarded. We would've probably had some great sex for a couple of months but never opened up enough for it to last. Getting to know each other the way we did over email and such a long stretch of time let us both open up in a way we never could've in real life."

Jackie shrugged. "Maybe. But looking back I certainly wish I'd spent those years with Dave instead of running away from him."

"I hear ya, sister."

Jackie stared out the window as they made their way back towards the house, remembering all the happy times she'd had with Dave, and wishing she could go back to her younger self and shake some sense into her.

But...

Melody was probably right. Those five years between their first night together and when Jackie finally stopped running from how she felt for him, had defined their relationship as much as the five they'd actually spent together.

CHAPTER 21

That night, Jackie lay in bed, staring at the ceiling, unable to sleep even though she was completely exhausted. Her mind just wouldn't let go. And it was threatening to dwell on Dave and all she'd lost.

Again.

She was so tired of circling his memory over and over and over again. But she couldn't seem to break free of it. At least not on her own. She'd had a glimmer of hope the last few days between all the time spent traveling and then the party and the day out with Melody. But alone in the dark, all the sorrow came back, smothering her so she could barely breathe.

She punched the mattress, wanting to get over this. Enough already.

C.K. Carr

But she couldn't. Not yet it seemed.

The creak of a board on the porch startled her. She sat up, waiting for some crazy intruder to bust through her door. But when the only sound that followed was the gentle rocking of the porch swing, she realized it must be George settling in for the night.

She sat there in the dark, debating what to do.

She could continue to lie there by herself, staring at the ceiling for half the night, hating herself for not being strong enough to move on already. Or she could join George on the porch and hope that his steady presence helped keep the darkness at bay until she was finally ready to sleep.

She hesitated a moment, wondering if she really wanted George to see her like this. He was a good friend, he'd known Dave for years, she trusted him implicitly. But grief was such a personal thing. It unlocked your deepest, darkest self. And she wasn't sure she wanted anyone else, no matter how good a friend, to see that.

Especially if, heaven forbid, she started crying. Again. Like always.

130

And what about him? Would he really want her to intrude on his solitude? He'd always hidden behind laughter and jokes, never sharing anything too deep. All those years she'd known him and he'd never once mentioned that his dad was dead. Maybe he wanted to be alone with his grief.

But if he had, he wouldn't have told her about how he sat out there each night. Maybe he needed her company as much as she needed his. They didn't need to talk about what they'd lost or how they were feeling, they could just sit together and silently share their burden.

Remind one another that they weren't alone.

Taking a deep breath for courage, she grabbed a sweatshirt Aidan had loaned her, threw it on over the t-shirt and shorts she'd been using for pajamas, and walked to the door.

CHAPTER 22

Jackie felt better about her choice when George greeted her with a smile and wave.

"Mind if I join you?" she asked, inching closer.

"Not at all. Want one?" He held up a beer. There was a full cooler at his feet.

She hesitated—it was already after midnight—but finally nodded. It might make them both feel more comfortable. And she didn't have to drink it, just hold it so she had something to do with her hands. "Sure. Thanks."

He pulled a bottle from the cooler, opened it, and handed it over, shifting to the end of the swing to give her enough space to sit down. She took a swig, not even tasting the beer, and sat on the very edge of the swing, too tense to lean back.

George lounged in his spot, arm thrown casually over the back of the swing. "Couldn't sleep either, huh?"

"No. I'm exhausted, but…Nights are the worst aren't they?"

"Yeah. I can't believe how little sleep I get these days." He laughed softly. "Of course, other times all I want to do is go to bed, bury myself under the covers, and sleep for days."

"I did that. For months." She took another swig of the beer.

"Did it help?"

She shook head. "No. Not at all. If you find out what does, you let me know." She finally leaned back.

It was a nice night, only a handful of clouds in the sky, a gentle breeze blowing through the trees. Water crashed against the shore somewhere in the distance and insects chirred nearby. The air smelled crisp and clean, just water and vegetation. She inhaled deeply, taking it all in, and caught the hint of George's aftershave or deodorant—something spicy but familiar.

They sat together in silence for a while, drinking their beers as George slowly rocked the swing back and forth with his foot. Finally, Jackie broke the silence, her thoughts once more straying too dangerously close to Dave. "It's beautiful here."

"That it is."

"And you said you bought this place?"

He took a long, deep swallow of his beer. "Yep. I was just renting it, but Nellie wanted a home. And this was perfect. Close enough to her family for her to see them regularly, but not so close they'd be here all the time. And she loved to run along that beach every morning." He shrugged one shoulder. "It's where we started, it seemed fitting it's where we should stay."

Jackie sensed a current of sorrow running below each of his words, but there was nothing in his tone or his face to show it. She shifted so she could study him. He continued to stare straight ahead, not looking at her, beer held casually in his hand. "It sounds like she was a remarkable woman," she said. "She'd have to be to settle GQ George down."

He bowed his head for a moment. "She was. Before her..." He shook his head. "I'd never really thought about the future, you know. I was young, I was having fun, seeing the world. A different port every season, a different girl every week. But she made me realize I wanted something more from life."

Jackie nodded.

"Not that I was going to move into the city and become an accountant or anything." He grinned at her, the moonlight shining on the scar on his cheek. "But having a partner to travel the world with? A woman who had the same zest and passion for life as I did?" He nodded. "That I could do."

He took a long swig of his beer. "Best of all, she actually wanted me, too."

Jackie laughed. "Pretty sure you never had a problem with that one. I seem to recall every single woman I knew throwing herself at you and you just picking and choosing which ones you wanted."

"Not every woman." He raised an eyebrow and held her gaze for a moment. "Plus, I'm getting older and uglier every day. Charm's bound to wear off sooner or later. Had to lock her down before it did."

"Now you sound like Dave. And you're both full of shit. What made him attractive, and what makes you so attractive to the ladies, isn't just your good looks."

He downed the rest of his beer. "You want another?"

"No, I'm good, thanks."

She bit her lip as he opened the new beer and took a big swallow, wondering where the line was between having a few beers to ease the night and having too many to drown the pain. The crowd they ran with had always been a heavy-partying group. Four, five, six beers a night was nothing. But somehow it was different when those beers were drunk alone in the dark in the middle of the night.

George caught her look and set his beer down next to the swing.

"You don't have to put that down because of me."

"Eh. It doesn't help anyway. I'd have to drink a case of beer before it actually did anything useful. It just gives me something to do while I'm sitting out here staring at nothing the whole night."

"So what do you do when someone like me isn't around to distract you?"

He shrugged. "Like I said, stare at nothing. Think about better times. I don't know. Figure it's a better view than the bedroom ceiling."

"That it is."

They settled into silence as she let the swing's steady rocking and George's presence soothe her. Eventually, as the night deepened and even the insects fell asleep, the chill became too much. Shivering, she stood. "I think I better get back inside before I catch cold."

George nodded, not really looking at her. "Thanks for keeping me company. I'm glad you're here. It…helps."

"Same." She shuffled back to her bedroom, finally relaxed enough to sleep.

But her dreams were a restless jumble of loss and need that left her even more tired.

CHAPTER 23

The next morning when Jackie stumbled out of bed it was just Melody waiting for her in the front room. She served Jackie up the remnants of a broccoli, bacon, and cheese quiche and a medley of fresh fruit still left over from the party.

"Today I thought we'd go for a hike," Melody declared as Jackie poured herself a cup of coffee.

"A hike? Aren't you jetlagged still? I am." Jackie sipped at the coffee, wondering how someone could have so much energy so early in the morning. And Melody didn't even drink coffee. How was that possible?

But then she realized that she'd been that way, too, once. Love. It had weird side effects. Plus, she saw that there

138

was already an empty Coke can sitting on the counter.

That must be the trick.

"It'll help work out the kinks," Melody said. "Plus, the forecast is threatening rain. If we don't get out today, who knows the next time we'll be able to."

"This is New Zealand. It's always raining or threatening to rain. But there's also always a window of nice weather somewhere in each day." She took a bite of the quiche. It was divine. Aidan had truly missed his calling.

"Hm. I don't know about that. I seem to recall walking in rain for my entire three-day hike of the Queen Charlotte Track."

"Was it uphill both ways, too?" Jackie teased.

Melody laughed. "No. But it was uphill a good portion of the time. And muddy. And all the locals kept passing me by like it was nothing. Have you ever compared their estimated walking time on a trail to how long it actually takes you? Or looked at their idea of what an easy trail is?"

"No. Can't say I have."

"You'll see today. Some track they describe as a half-hour nature hike for grandmothers will turn out to be an hour-long uphill scramble along a rocky trail with three river crossings thrown in just for fun and no bridges anywhere in sight."

Jackie laughed, but then she shook her head. "Seriously, Melody. I really don't know if I'm up for it. You forget how little I've done the last year."

"We'll start slow and work our way up then. But if we don't get started we can never work our way up."

Jackie winced and focused on eating more of the quiche. Melody was like a tank once she got going. There was no stopping her. This hike was going to happen whether Jackie wanted it to or not. Unless she got conveniently sick...

"And don't even think you can talk your way out of this with some lame excuse about not feeling well. I did not bring you here so you could spend the entire summer hiding in your bedroom."

"We just got here! Give me a few days, would you?"

"No." Melody smiled at her, arms crossed, smugly confident that she'd get her way.

Jackie glared her down as she continued to eat her meal, but by the end of it she hadn't managed to come up with one excuse good enough to convince Melody she needed to stay home for the day.

By ten o'clock they were at the trailhead, lunches packed, hiking boots and sunscreen on, cameras in hand, ready to explore the New Zealand countryside.

CHAPTER 24

That night when Jackie went out to the porch to sit with George, he nodded to a big blanket folded up on "her" side of the swing. "Figured you might be more comfortable with that."

"Thank you." She wrapped it around herself and curled up next to him. "Not all of us are used to hours spent out on the cold water."

"It's not always cold. Did Dave ever tell you about the season we worked Tahiti?"

"No. When was that?"

He grinned at her. "Not sure if it was the first time you left his sorry butt behind or the second. But he called me up and told me he needed to get as far away as he could from Dubrovnik and as soon as he could."

"The second time, then."

George nodded. "So I suggested Tahiti. A buddy had been having some success down there taking rich tourists out for little day cruises and he said we could set up shop without any pesky visa or business permit issues to worry about."

"And? Did that actually work?" Sailors were a casual lot sometimes when it came to foreign jurisdictions and rules, but those foreign jurisdictions weren't. She wasn't sure she knew a single sailor that hadn't been booted from at least one country for working without proper approval.

"Ahhh." He scratched behind his ear. "Let's just say we left town in a hurry a couple months later. But the time we spent there…Oh my. Beautiful. Of course, when you're sailing mate is a lovelorn fool who can't stop talking about the woman who left him just because he left her alone long enough to go to the market…"

Jackie blushed. "I was too young to be that in love."

He laughed. "You're never too young to be in love. I first fell in love when I was ten years old. With a girl named Elizabeth. She had long blonde hair and pretty blue eyes and she kissed me behind the bleachers one day after school. I would've done anything for her after that."

"Long blonde hair and pretty blue eyes? What a cliché you were."

"Hey! First love is first love. Don't mock that. I spent weeks pining after her, writing her bad poetry, bringing her little gifts..."

"I hope she appreciated it."

"No. I caught her laughing about one of my poems with a couple of her friends. Broke my heart. But, man, did I love that girl while it lasted."

"Was she your first kiss?"

"Mmhm. And for that I'll always love her. She opened my eyes to the beauty of a woman...How soft her lips could be and how wonderful it felt to run my fingers through her hair..." He stared off into the distance, a slight smile on his lips.

"That's when you became a complete dog isn't it? Didn't let another one tie you down until Nellie."

"Hey!" He mock-frowned at her. "I was not a dog. My mother raised me better than that. I treated every woman I ever kissed with complete honesty. I let her know right up front I wasn't going to stick around long, but that we could have fun while it lasted."

Jackie laughed. "You fool. Don't you realize that's catnip for some women? That whole, 'Baby, I'm bound to leave' shtick? You might've been being honest, but they were just seeing some good-looking man who'd never been truly loved before and would change his freewheeling ways if only he met the right woman. Them."

"Well, all I can say is I never lied about it. If they chose to see things differently, that's not my fault. And you know that works both directions don't you?" He gave her a pointed look. "Dave wasn't the only one you pulled your little disappearing act on if I recall correctly. I bought more than a few beers over the years for some poor confused fool who'd fallen under your spell and didn't know what to do when you picked up and left."

"Hey now."

"It's true. Remember Xavier? Or Chris? Or Pablo?"

She grimaced. "Sort of? Was Chris blonde?"

George laughed, a loud boisterous laugh like she remembered from the old days. "No, he had dark brown hair." He shook his head. "You were a heartbreaker back in the day. Still might be. Kev seems quite taken with you."

"Kev?" She couldn't help blushing. "He's fun to flirt with. And doesn't know about Dave, so it's easy to forget for a bit, you know?"

He nodded. "Yeah. I get that. I can flirt with my guests. Just enough to make things fun, but not so much they think there's something there. And then they move on the next day. It's perfect."

She bit her lip. "You haven't told Kev, have you? I don't want..."

"No. Not my place. And Aidan won't either." He elbowed her gently. "Just try not to break the guy's heart, would you? He's a good mate to have around in a pinch."

"It's just flirting."

"Sure it is. Just be sure he knows that, too."

They continued laughing and teasing one another, reminiscing about old times until Jackie started yawning uncontrollably and she couldn't keep her eyes open.

George nudged her leg. "Better pack it in for the night."

"Are you sure? I can stay out here and keep you company a bit longer."

"Actually, I think I'll head in, too. Get a few hours of rest in a real bed before morning. Turns out sleeping on this thing with my head thrown back isn't all that great for my old bones."

They both stood, staring at each other awkwardly for a moment.

Jackie folded up the blanket and handed it back to him. "Well, then. Good night."

"Good night."

As Jackie let herself back into her room she realized she was smiling. It was good to spend time with George. He knew her. And Dave. And he understood enough not to push, to just be there for her.

It was nice, too, to know she could do the same for him.

CHAPTER 25

The next afternoon Jackie took the opportunity to get away from the house for a walk of the neighborhood. It wasn't that she didn't like spending time with Melody, but it was a big adjustment to go from spending all of her time alone to suddenly living with three people, all of whom were keeping an eye on her to make sure she was doing okay.

It was exhausting.

Plus, Melody actually had things she needed to do. That was obvious by the way she pulled out her laptop almost as soon as Jackie said she was going for a walk. (After making sure Jackie didn't want company, of course. Heaven forbid Jackie be left alone for a moment...)

She strolled down the street, breathing in the fresh spring air, and admiring the cute little houses—what she could see behind flowering bushes and trees. New Zealand was so green. This time of year in Tahoe the grass would still be brown and dry, but every house she passed had a thriving lawn covered in lush green grass and someone was mowing their yard nearby, the steady drone of the mower the only sound other than the birds in the trees.

It was different than California, but she could get used to it. She'd slathered sunscreen on, though, because as deceptively nice as it was, she knew there was much more risk of sunburn here than back home even if it was a lower elevation.

As she strolled along the street, trying not to let her mind drift too far in any dangerous direction, she wished she'd remembered to bring her iPod. It was so quiet, so peaceful. No distractions to keep her mind from Dave or George or...

Kev?

She narrowed her eyes as she continued walking towards the man a few houses down mowing his yard. He had his shirt off and his back to her, but she was pretty sure it was him. She let herself admire his sun-tanned body from his muscular arms to his long legs to his nice ass. The short shorts he was wearing didn't leave a whole lot to the imagination, which was fine with her although it still sort of amazed her that men in other countries still wore shorts like that.

Not that she was complaining...

He turned to come back in her direction and saw her. The lawn mower sputtered to a stop, and he waved at her, flashing a big grin. "Hey, Jackie. Come to watch me sweat in the hot midday sun?" He sauntered towards her.

She figured he deserved as good as he got and moved her sunglasses to the top of her head so she could blatantly ogle him. "What can I say? It's a hard job, but somebody has to do it. Surprised given how short those shorts are that you felt the need to wear any clothes at all."

He laughed. "The neighbors complain when I'm starkers. Don't know why. I think I look pretty good." He leaned closer. "You ever want to do some naked sunbathing, just drop by. Be happy to join you."

"You sure the neighbors won't complain?"

"Nah. Not if you're there." He nodded to the house on the right. "Four kayak guides live there. All men. And three bus guides live there. Also, all men."

"Ah, now I see the problem."

"Yep. They can't handle the competition. Bring some lady friend home and there I am in all my naked glory and the ladies just can't look at anyone else after that." He winked.

Jackie laughed.

"Care for a beer? I could use a bit of a break."

She was tempted. But she wasn't quite ready for things to go past a little bit of flirting, so she shook her head. "Rain check? I want to get back and showered before the boys finish up their afternoon cruise."

He stared at her, open-mouthed. "Can it be?"

"What?"

"A woman who can resist my incredible charm?" He shook his head slightly, smiling at her with a wicked grin. "I'm going to have to up my game."

"No, you don't."

"So you do want me, then?"

"I...You know, I need to get going." She nodded towards the yard. "And you need to get back to work. That lawn isn't going to mow itself."

"Yes, ma'am. But someday you will let me buy you a beer, won't you?"

"Of course."

As she walked away, she felt a little lighter on her feet. Kev wasn't her ideal man by any stretch but it was fun to have someone to banter with. And maybe more? Someday. But not today.

CHAPTER 26

That night Aidan made steaks on the grill and they ate outside, talking and laughing and drinking wine late into the night, swapping stories of all of their crazy misadventures around the world.

Like the time Aidan hit on a woman in a bar in Thailand only to find out "she" was a "he." And the time George had to fast-talk his way out of being arrested in Mexico because he'd made the mistake of spending the night drinking with a guy who turned out to be a drug mule.

Melody's stories were less wild, but it seemed she'd had to fend off any number of strange but ardent admirers around the world, including a few that had followed her for blocks on end trying to convince her to give them a chance.

Jackie's stories tended more towards skinny-dipping with people she didn't know well or picking up and taking off to some new country on the spur of the moment. (Because unlike Melody, if a man had stopped her in the street and told her she was beautiful she would've given him a listen before running away and pretending she didn't speak his language. That's how a few of those spur-of-the-moment trips had started, after all.)

It was a great night.

And later, after everyone else had gone to bed, she snuck out to the porch to join George. They were both happy and tired, so they didn't talk much. They just sat together, listening to the quiet of the night, and keeping one another company.

She did tell him about her encounter with Kev, though.

He shook his head.

"What?"

"You're going to break his heart."

"That boy doesn't have a heart to break. He's the world's biggest flirt."

"Well, you're going to break his spirit then. Make him doubt his natural prowess with women."

She snorted. "I seem to recall you being an outrageous flirt back in the day and I didn't break you."

"That's because I was too smart to let you."

"What's that mean?"

"It means I knew better than to do more than trade a few witty lines back and forth with you before I moved on to someone who wouldn't leave me bruised and broken."

She slapped his arm. "That is not fair. Name one man I left bruised and broken."

"Dave. The first time. The second time. The third time. The..."

"Okay, fine. Dave is one, but that was it."

"And Michael the Greek. Remember him?"

"Ohhh. I do." She bit her lip. "He wasn't that bad off after. Was he?"

George laughed. "The boy sang Greek love songs to himself for a week while drinking ouzo in the corner."

"No! He didn't."

George nodded.

"Really?"

"Mmhm. See? You didn't even pay enough attention to him after to know."

"Well, I won't break Kev like that, okay? I'm just having fun flirting. It's nice to have someone around who doesn't know all the shit in my life."

He nodded and took a sip of his beer.

She studied him for a long moment, feeling slightly trembly as she added, "But it's also nice to have someone who gets exactly what I'm going through."

"Ah, not sure that's even possible."

"Maybe not. But it's still nice to have you to talk to if I need it." She waited for him to look at her and smiled when he did.

He patted her knee. "Yeah. Same."

They settled back into silence.

As he slowly rocked the swing, though, she realized that as much as she enjoyed spending those late-night hours with him, he really hadn't talked about Nellie or the accident. He'd let her talk about Dave, but he was still holding back, protecting himself.

Something Gained

That was okay. If he ever did want to talk about it, Jackie would be there for him the way he'd been there for her.

Because that's what friends were for.

CHAPTER 27

The next couple weeks passed in a blur.

Between Melody, Aidan, and George, Jackie rarely had time to think and she certainly didn't have time to mope around missing Dave. Melody dragged her out on a hike at least once per day, sometimes twice if the weather was nice enough.

And Aidan kept to his promise and stuffed her full of delicious food. From his famous stuffed French toast to fresh-caught snapper to good-old-fashioned steaks, he kept her plate full of deliciousness. And on the few occasions he wasn't around to cook, George stepped in. By the end of the second week she had already outgrown her kiddie clothes and had to buy a whole new set of shorts and t-shirts.

Ones that, thankfully, weren't covered in cartoon characters.

George and Aidan went out sailing most days except for when the weather refused to cooperate, but they almost always were back in time for dinner. And afterwards the four of them sat around talking or playing card games until it grew too late or Melody and Aidan started making soulful longing looks at one another and she and George chased them off.

And at night, after everyone else was asleep and the only sounds were the ocean waves lapping against the shore or a late-night storm pattering against the roof, she and George sat together on the porch swing sharing silence, laughter, or memories depending on their mood.

They talked about Dave a lot. George had spent more time with him than she'd known and he was full of stories about Dave getting into one scrape or another and needing rescued, or of George getting into one and needing Dave's help. George's stories filled in gaps she'd never known existed.

He was a good listener, too. Jackie found herself talking about those last five years she'd spent with Dave once she'd stopped running. And about the future they'd thought they'd have.

And George finally started to open up and talk about Nellie. When he did, his eyes would light up and his voice would fill with love. It broke Jackie's heart to see what he'd lost.

She offered what comfort she could, listening when he wanted to talk, letting the matter rest when he didn't. And she took comfort in the support he offered, grateful that there was someone she could talk to who'd known Dave and didn't immediately change the subject when he came up.

Slowly, with each passing day, Jackie felt a little bit stronger and more ready to face the world again. Between Aidan, Melody, and George they showed her that she could still laugh and enjoy life, that it wasn't all blackness and sorrow.

She still missed Dave. And she always would. That was just part of who she was now.

But, finally, she could see something past the blackness that had almost drowned her.

It helped, too, that she crossed paths with Kev a few more times and that he was even more outrageously flirtatious with her than before. She still wasn't ready to go there, but it was nice to think she could.

CHAPTER 28

Jackie lay in her bed listening to the soft sound of the wind blowing through the trees and the waves crashing against the shore. George and Aidan were still out on a full-moon charter they ran once a month, so no George to keep the dark thoughts at bay.

She was restless, unable to sleep, her mind a whirl of thoughts she couldn't track. She was trying very hard to live one day at a time, to not look too far into the future or the past but just focus on this special time she'd been given with her friends.

But alone in the dark she couldn't keep the questions away any longer.

What came next? This idyll couldn't last forever. At some point she'd have to return to her old life or forge a new one. And where was that going to be? What was she going to do?

She couldn't follow Aidan and Melody around for the rest of her life. Eventually they'd want their own space. And she couldn't just sit on the porch talking to George forever either. Eventually he too would move on and recover, find a new love or perhaps a long string of lovers, and leave her behind.

Her stomach clenched at the thought of being alone again. Of having to make it through an entire, dark night with no one there to comfort her.

She needed a plan or else she'd just sink back to where she'd been before. Her thoughts strayed dangerously close to an empty house full of memories and days spent stewing in grief.

She couldn't go back to that. She'd lost too many months already drowning in her sorrow.

But if not there, then where?

She was fortunate enough to have money to go wherever she wanted but unfortunate enough to not know where that was.

When it finally became clear she wasn't going to fall asleep anytime soon, she sat up. Maybe a late-night stroll would clear her mind. She paused on the porch to inhale air that still carried the tang of a late afternoon storm. New Zealand was so green, so lushly beautiful, so alive—unlike the stark, dry beauty of home. Not that she'd ever thought of Tahoe as stark or dry before coming here, but it really was.

In comparison.

She strolled to the beach, savoring the sight of a full moon above her and the water slowly lapping at the shore. As her feet sank into the soft sand along the water's edge, she lifted her face, letting the cool silver light of the moon shine upon her as a light breeze tugged at her hair. It wasn't going to rain again, but there was still that hint of storminess to the night that made her skin tingle.

She closed her eyes and held her arms wide, breathing deeply and relishing the moment. The peace, the comfort. Coming to this place had truly been the right choice. She was still fragile, but the cracks were starting to heal, and she could now enjoy a moment like this without tears or a hollow feeling of loss dragging her under.

She sighed, wishing Dave were there to share the moment, but the thought didn't make her cry like it would have even a month ago. It still made her sad, but that was a part of her now. She'd finally accepted that she'd never be who she'd been before. Never be able to go back to that carefree girl who'd danced on the tabletops in a dive bar in Dubrovnik, full of life and passion and the promise of love.

She might still dance on a tabletop someday, but she'd always know that the music could end at any moment, always carry that small piece of darkness with her now.

As she walked along the beach she finally realized that she needed to grieve as much for herself as for Dave. For who she'd been and could never be again. That didn't mean her life had to end, though. She knew that now, too.

She strolled along the beach, pretending Dave was there with her, just out of sight, sharing the calm beauty of the night, telling one of his stupid jokes that made her laugh even as she groaned. She talked to him softly, telling him about the last few weeks and listening to his imagined responses.

It was a pleasant time spent with his loving memory—something she'd needed without realizing it. To know that he was always there in spirit if she needed him. That she didn't have to push thoughts of him away all the time, but could embrace them and enjoy them instead.

She reached the end of the beach and turned back towards the house, at peace, rested, ready to live in the moment and not worry about what came next or what she'd lost.

She flexed her hand, wishing Dave really was there to tuck his hand in hers and hold her in his arms as she slept.

Maybe, sometime, sooner rather than later, she'd be ready to let another man stand there holding her hand.

But not yet.

CHAPTER 29

When she returned to the house, George was sitting on the porch swing in the dark, a beer in hand. The lights inside the house were off—Aidan must already be in bed. She waved to him as she crossed the yard and he waved back, but neither one broke the silence as she made her way to his side.

He moved over and patted the swing. "I thought you were already asleep. Want a beer?"

She shook her head and sat down next to him, moving the blanket aside. After the cool of the ocean, the heat of his body was like a furnace warming the air around them. "I tried to go to sleep, but seems I'm too used to sitting out here with you these days. So I went for a walk instead."

He nodded towards the beach. "You should be careful. You never know who you might run into."

She laughed softly. "Here? This is one of the safest places I've ever been. I didn't even see anyone."

"All it takes is one crazy, you know. And there're lots of tourists who rent bachs around here so it's constantly changing. You get one drunk fool who won't take no and..." He shook his head.

"Yes, father."

He snorted. "You sound just like Nellie. She was always reminding me that she was perfectly capable of taking care of herself. Which is why those moments when she let me help were so special."

They talked softly for the next hour, the conversation moving from Nellie and her fierce independent streak to Dave and the few times he'd tried to help Jackie when she was seriously determined to do something on her own and how poorly that had gone.

Jackie realized as she watched George talking that he too was starting to heal. He still had a beer or two when he was sitting on the porch, but she no longer felt that warning in her gut that told her he was trying to drown his sorrow. And he smiled more. Really smiled, not just pretended.

"What?" He narrowed his eyes at her.

"Nothing."

"No, no, no. It was something. Out with it." He stared her down, his lips curved into a half-smile that she couldn't help but match.

"I was just thinking."

"That's obvious. What about?"

She bit her lip. Would saying the words, calling it out, somehow change things? She hoped not. "I was just thinking that...that you're looking better. Happier than you were when I arrived."

He sat up straighter and looked away from her, out into the night.

"I'm sorry. I didn't mean to upset you."

"No. It's fine. You're right. I am." The warmth was gone from his voice.

She reached out to touch his arm, but he jerked away from her.

"That's not a bad thing, George. To feel some happiness."

"You're right. It's not." He still wouldn't look at her.

"Do you...Do you want to talk about it?"

"No." He stood abruptly, causing the swing to jerk backwards and forwards again.

Jackie braced herself, staring up at him in surprise. "George? If I said something wrong, I'm sorry."

He shook his head, still not looking at her. "You didn't. I just...I need to be alone." He walked away, never looking back, headed for the beach.

She stood, wondering if she should go after him or not. But she knew that if their positions were reversed, she wouldn't want someone chasing after her.

Sighing, she watched him disappear into the trees.

She wrapped the blanket around her shoulders, wishing he'd come back. She hadn't meant to hurt him. But sometimes grief was like skating on an iced-over lake. You never knew when the ice would break and drag you back under.

She shivered as she stood there alone, realizing how much she needed him to come back. Needed his calm, steady presence to remind her she wasn't alone.

She couldn't hold back the tears as she stared into the darkness where he'd disappeared. She turned away. She didn't want him to see her like that.

She stumbled to her room and curled up under the covers, finally letting the flood gates open and the sorrow that was still there, lurking right under the surface, claim her.

CHAPTER 30

Jackie slept until noon the next day, grateful that Melody didn't try to wake her earlier. She wasn't actually asleep the whole time, she just couldn't bring herself to get up and face the day. Somehow she'd hurt George and she didn't know how to fix it.

She needed him. Desperately. She hadn't realized until the night before how much he'd been holding her steady all these weeks. How much she'd needed their late night talks.

And now...

She closed her eyes and forced herself to get up. It was probably fine. George would be there tonight and they could go back to how things had been and pretend she'd never pointed out to him how much better he was.

When she made her way to the living room, Melody was there, working on her laptop and she asked, "Did you see George after he got home last night?"

"No. Why?"

She didn't know why she hadn't told Melody or Aidan about the late night talks she had with George, but they felt like something private that she shouldn't share without his permission.

"I don't know. It's weird. He left first thing this morning before Aidan was even up. Said he was making a run to Auckland for a few days and suggested Aidan use Kev to help him out with the bigger charters."

"Is Kev even available to help?"

"Yeah, he had some sort of motor trouble, I guess, and his boat is out of commission for a week or so. But, still. Aidan's worried. Said he's been awfully quiet the last week or so. Brooding almost."

"Really?" Jackie helped herself to some leftover pancakes and bacon. George had been more animated than ever the last week... "Huh."

Melody set aside her laptop and stared at Jackie, eyes narrowed.

"Alright. Out with it. What aren't you telling me?"

"Nothing."

"Jackie..."

She jabbed her fork into another bite of pancakes. "I said it was nothing."

"George up and disappears on the same day you decide to sleep until noon. Your eyes are all red and puffy which means you've been crying. And the way you responded to my comment about George brooding implied you don't agree. But it's nothing. Out with it. You two hooking up?"

"What? No. What made you think that?"

"This isn't the biggest house, you know. Sometimes we hear you and George laughing after we've gone to bed. I never said anything because it wasn't my business. But...Do you need to talk about it?"

"It really is nothing. George can't sleep most nights and neither can I. So we sit out on the porch and talk. Have been pretty much every night since I arrived." She shrugged one shoulder. "It's been good. For both of us. But that's all it is."

"And the last week?"

"Has been just like the other nights since I arrived. We talk, we laugh. A lot of times we talk about Dave. Turns out George crewed with him more than I'd realized and has a ton of funny stories about him. A few times we've talked about Nellie." She pushed her plate away. She wasn't hungry anymore.

Melody glanced at it, but didn't say anything, which was a nice change from the first week Jackie had been there.

"So what changed last night?" Melody opened a tin of shortbread cookies and pushed them towards Jackie after taking a couple for herself.

"It was nothing. Or it should've been nothing. I just happened to mention to him that he was a lot happier these days than when I arrived."

"And?

"He clammed up and then went for a walk on the beach. Said he needed to be alone."

"And you?"

"I let him go."

"So where do the tears come in?"

Jackie grabbed a cookie and took a bite.

"Jackie?"

"I don't know. I...Watching him walk away like that, I started crying. And then it just, I couldn't stop it once I'd started. You know how it can be."

Melody nodded. "Yeah. It just comes over you sometimes, doesn't it?" She bit her lip. "But this thing with George..."

"What about it?"

"Well...The way he reacted last night and the way he's been brooding during the days when he's not around you...And the way you teared up when he walked away...Do you think...Are there feelings there?"

"No. Don't be ridiculous. We're just friends." She dumped the rest of the pancakes in the trash and put her plate in the sink. "Why does everyone always assume that if a man and a woman enjoy spending time together that it has to be romantic?"

Melody held her hands up in surrender. "It was just a question. Sorry I asked."

"Yeah, well. Don't ask it again, okay?"

She turned away. She needed a shower.

CHAPTER 31

The shower didn't help. All Jackie did the whole time was go back over all her conversations with George looking for signs that maybe he thought it was more than just two friends spending time together.

Nothing. No attempts to touch her, no sexual comments, no questions about whether she was ready to date again.

Just friendship.

Just freely offered conversation and comfort.

Melody was wrong. She didn't get it. She didn't understand that grief could hollow you out so there was nothing left inside. No desire, no need. Nothing.

George was just upset to realize that he was finally starting to move past his grief a bit. Fair enough. It made **her** a little uncomfortable to realize how much she'd laughed and actually enjoyed herself since she'd arrived here. Like it was somehow a betrayal of what she'd had with Dave.

She was glad she'd moved past the dark place she'd been in when she came to New Zealand, but there was still that lingering loyalty to his memory. That belief that if she loved him as much as she'd thought she did that she should never be able to let go and find happiness again.

Maybe George felt a bit of that, too. Guilt for being happy when the woman he'd loved was gone forever.

As she toweled off, she realized that she couldn't spend the night wondering where George was and if he was okay. She made her way back to the living room where Melody sat with her laptop propped on her knees, typing away.

She leaned against the wall. "Hey, so I was thinking..."

"Yeah?"

"You want to go out? Like, night on the town, out?"

"Really?" Melody sounded so surprised, Jackie almost took it back.

"Yeah, I think it would be nice. Get out. Enjoy a little of the local scene."

"Sure. Don't see why not. I'll text Aidan and tell him we'll meet him in town. The pub serves some pretty good food from what I've heard."

"Great."

"Of course…If we're going to drink tonight we need to get in some exercise this morning. What do you think about hiking over to Cathedral Cove and getting some photos in?"

Jackie groaned. "Don't you ever have days where you just want to sit around doing nothing?"

"No. Not here. It's too beautiful. So? Up for it?"

Jackie sighed. "Yeah, sure."

It beat sitting around the house thinking about George.

"Good. I'll get in a shower. Be ready to leave in half an hour."

As Melody bounded down the hallway, Jackie trudged back to her room. She just knew Melody was going to spend the whole day asking about her late-night conversations with George and she really didn't want to talk about it. Not one bit.

CHAPTER 32

Jackie spent the entire hike to the cove tensed for Melody's questions about George, but they never came. Instead she chattered about the latest photo spread she'd pitched to National Geographic and whether it was going to rain later and how the neighbor had come by the day before and offered them some homemade biltong which seemed to be a form of jerky but how Melody wasn't sure she wanted to try it because the guy said he'd made it in his closet and how on earth could that be hygienic.

She didn't even pause long enough for Jackie to respond, just bounced from topic to topic to topic. Which was fine. Jackie wasn't up for talking anyway. Instead she let her body fall into the rhythm of hiking and navigating the muddy paths at a steady pace that kept her grounded enough not to think too much about George or Dave or much of anything at all.

The path was washed out right before the end and they had to navigate a muddy hillside that threatened to disappear under their feet at any moment, but when they finally made it down to the beach, the famous arch was as stunningly beautiful as in all the movies.

"I can't believe in all our hiking this last month that we never made it here before," Jackie said.

"I know." Melody took her camera from her pack and started adjusting the settings, glancing at the sky to judge the light. "But there are always so many tourists and it's not like it's a unique shot. I figured it was better to wander some of the lesser known trails instead. I'm going to set this on a one-hour exposure to see if I can get a shot without people in it. That okay with you?"

Jackie nodded as she pulled out her own camera. Melody tended towards nature photography but Jackie preferred to take photos of actual people. She focused on a pair of Japanese tourists who'd just arrived, and snapped a few shots. The girl had kitten heels on, a short skirt, and was carrying an actual purse. How she'd navigated that muddy stretch of path, Jackie didn't want to know, but she had and somehow managed to still look completely flawless, not a speck of mud on her.

Jackie glanced around for others to photograph, but her heart wasn't really in it, so she tucked the camera back in her pack and waited for Melody to finish setting up. They found a rock shelf nearby out of the path of the crowds and climbed up to sit.

When they were all settled in, Melody turned to her with a deliberate sigh. "Well...Now that we've got some time, I guess we should talk about what's going on with you and George."

"The whole way here I was expecting you to bring it up, but now I see you were just lulling me into dropping my guard first."

"I'm good that way." Melody grinned. "Look. Tell me as much or as little as you want, I won't push, but I should remind you that I can be a pretty good listener and sometimes it helps to talk these things through."

Jackie watched the groups of tourists wandering the beach looking for anything else to photograph other than the arch, but there wasn't a whole lot else to see. Made her wonder why so many thought the hike to get there was worth it. Then again, no one really knew that's all there was until they'd already done it and then they had an amazing photo to show their friends and their friends probably saw it and wanted to get one of their own and on and on it went.

Melody sat next to her, quietly waiting.

Finally, Jackie gave up.

If she didn't talk about it now, it would hang there between them until she did. "Honestly, I never really thought of George and me as anything other than good friends. Not until you said something this morning. And I still don't think it's more than that. He's a friend and he knew Dave and he isn't scared of talking about him, which is nice. You and Aidan try so hard to avoid the topic it's almost comical. So to be able to sit there at night with George and just laugh and remember what Dave was like...It feels good."

Melody nodded. "Do you think he thinks there's more there?"

"No." Once again, Jackie thought back over all of their conversations. "There's nothing in what he's said or done to indicate he's feeling anything more than friendship for me. You know what guys are like when they're interested. There's always this hovering thing about them, like they're just waiting for you to give them some sign they'd have a chance so they can act."

Melody wrinkled her nose in agreement.

"But there's none of that with him. He never tries to sit too close. He never gets all touchy with me. He doesn't search my face for some clue I'm interested. Or try to direct the conversation towards any of that. He's just...there. Listening to me, telling his stories."

Jackie chewed on her thumbnail as she thought about it. "I don't want to lose that. I...I've really come a long way since I arrived. And he's a big part of it."

"You have. I didn't want to say anything, because I didn't want to freak you out, but the transformation has been amazing. I mean, you don't even look like a scarecrow anymore."

Jackie rolled her eyes. "Thanks for that."

"Someone had to say it."

"Well, anyway. I think my talks with George have had a lot to do with how well I'm doing. To know I don't have to hide my grief. That I can miss Dave but still laugh and enjoy life a bit…" She wrung her hands together. "And I think it's been good for him, too. Those first few nights I sat out there he had this big cooler of beer with him and I got the impression he'd been drinking that much each and every night. But after I started joining him he's had just one beer. Maybe two. No more than that."

"Yeah, Aidan noticed that. He didn't know the cause, but he said George was back in the game the last couple weeks. That he'd been kind of fuzzy before and Aidan had needed to keep a close eye on things to make sure he didn't hurt himself or anyone else, but that something had finally shifted."

Jackie stared out at the ocean, chewing on her thumbnail until she noticed and shoved her hand under her thigh.

"So what do you think changed last night?" Melody asked. "Why'd he get so upset?"

"I think..." She pressed her lips together, working through it as she spoke. "I think he hadn't realized how much he'd improved. And when I pointed it out to him..." She shrugged. "I think maybe he felt guilty about it? Like he shouldn't be enjoying that time with me? Like it was somehow a betrayal to Nellie's memory?" She shook her head. "But it wasn't. No more than my enjoying our time together was a betrayal of Dave. We were **honoring** their memories."

"It's probably hard for him to see that. And it hasn't been as long for him as it's been for you."

"I know. I just wish there were something I could do to make it better."

Melody hugged her close for a second. "Just give it time. He'll come around."

Jackie nodded, drawing her knees up to her chest and resting her chin on them. She hoped Melody was right, because she wasn't sure she could do this without him.

CHAPTER 33

Jackie tried texting George later in the day, but he never responded so she figured she just had to let it go and hope he'd be back soon and that things wouldn't have shifted between them too much. As she dressed for dinner—actually putting on a bit of makeup for the first time since she'd arrived—she thought about how much she hated grief.

It was the worst feeling ever. It twisted you around in so many ways. Filling you with guilt and loneliness and despair.

It sucked and she hated it.

But all she could do was make it through each day and hope that little by little she could get better until it was just some distant reminder of the past

188

and not this ever-present looming presence in her life.

She and Melody met Aidan at the pub at six. As soon as they walked through the door, Jackie knew it was going to be an interesting night, because Kev was there, too.

"Jackie, at last I can buy you that beer you've been promising to let me buy you." He held his arms wide and she let him hug her, raising an eyebrow at Aidan over his shoulder.

"Hope you don't mind that I invited Kev to join us. He was helping out with my afternoon charter."

"Oh, that's right. I'd forgotten your boat's out of action. What happened to it?

She settled into the booth across from Aidan and Melody. Kev slid in next to her, his thigh resting against hers as he launched into the story of how a few too many beers and an unfortunate use of a wrench had led to the demise of his engine. It was a funny story, but made her realize even more that Kev was one of those types of sailors who were fun to love, but easy to leave. Always one foolish decision from disaster and often living on someone's couch because they'd caught a bad break.

Not like Aidan who had everything buttoned up. Or...George. She wished he were there, but nothing to be done about it now. And Kev was a nice, good-looking guy. And a definite flirt. He kept her laughing the whole night as he made over the top jokes about his prowess both on the water and off, all the while with that look that let her know he was interested if she was.

She enjoyed their banter, poking his ego every chance she got, but she wasn't interested in anything more than that. Not tonight.

He didn't seem to mind, taking her subtle rejection in stride and promising her as the night wound down that when she did change her mind he'd be ready and waiting. He left around midnight with a flourished bow and kiss of her hand like some sort of prince charming.

As soon as he was out of earshot, Aidan leaned forward. "You know, Jackie, we're not your parents. You want to go stay at that young man's house, you feel free to do so."

"You know damned well that if I wanted to go home with him I would've. With or without your permission."

"I'm just sayin'...He seemed awfully fond of you. And he's a good bloke."

"I know, but I'm not quite there yet. I'm sure Melody already told you about my one disastrous attempt to do something like that?"

He scratched at his ear. "She may have mentioned something."

"Well...It taught me not to push these things. Seems I'm not the same hoyden I once was."

"Ah, that's gonna break all the boys' hearts when they find out." He winked at her and she laughed.

Melody, who'd definitely had one too many drinks, leaned forward, staring Jackie down. "Don't you miss it?"

"Miss what?"

"Sex." She glanced over at Aidan and then back to Jackie. "I'm telling you, if I lost Aidan...I don't know what I'd do. I'd have to find someone..."

Aidan roared, his loud guffaw drawing eyes from everyone in the bar. "Says the girl who hadn't exactly been with anyone for a while prior to meeting me. And now you're going to what? Run out and find someone new before I'm even buried in my grave?"

"Well, you know...It's easy to go without if enough time has passed. But once you get that taste and remember what it's like...It's kind of like quitting Coke. I don't think I could do it now."

Jackie covered her ears and shook her head from side to side saying "na-na-na" over and over again as Aidan started to respond. They both stopped and stared at her until she removed her hands.

"Jackie, what on earth are you doing?"

"The last thing I want to hear about right now is you two's sex life."

He shrugged. "Fine, fine, fine. I guess I won't tell you about..."

She did it again until he stopped.

When she once again removed her hands, he mock-frowned at her. "Never known you to be such a prude before, Jackie."

"Well, you've never known me to not be with someone before either, now have you?"

"Fair enough." He nodded towards the door. "You sure you don't want to go running after Kev? He'd fix you right up and then you could be the one telling us too much."

"I'm sure. Can we go home now?"

They made their way outside, laughing and talking the whole way home.

Jackie had actually forgotten about the whole George thing until they pulled into the empty driveway and it all came rushing back. There must've been something of what she was feeling on her face, because Aidan gave her a quick hug as they walked inside. "It'll be okay. Just give him a day or two to come around."

She nodded, hoping he was right, but worried he wasn't.

CHAPTER 34

George didn't return until late the next day after everyone was already in bed. Jackie, who was lying in bed, unable to sleep, heard him arrive and go straight to his room. She waited, body tensed, to hear the sound of him out on the porch, but it never came.

As the hours ticked by, she wondered how to repair what she'd broken, tears falling silently down her cheeks and soaking into the pillow until it was a wet mess and she knew there was no chance she'd be able to sleep on it even if she wanted to.

She finally gave up pretending, threw on a sweatshirt, and snuck outside. She crept along the porch, rushing past the empty swing, fighting to keep the tears back as she made her way towards the steps. She winced as she stepped on the squeaky board, but kept going, sure that George wouldn't move from his room no matter what he heard.

It was a dark night, the sky full of clouds and the wind brisk enough to blow her hair in her face. She pushed on towards the beach. She didn't know why she was out there alone in the dark and the cold, but she just couldn't stay in that room another moment.

She walked along the beach. The waves crashed against the shore and she startled at every sound, sure that George's boogeyman was going to get her. Gone was the peaceful moonlit feeling she'd had the last time she walked the beach at night. Now she was just tense and unhappy, her mind a swirl of emotions—disappointment, sorrow, anger.

She turned back halfway down the beach, shivering from the chill of the impending storm and wet from the spray of the ocean.

As she came closer to the path to the house, she froze. There was someone standing there, hidden within the trees, watching her.

She looked around.

She was completely alone.

And the wind was blowing strong enough no one would hear her scream.

She bit her lip, not knowing what to do next.

Maybe the man would leave if she just stayed where she was. But she was so cold and she really wanted to get back inside.

Just as she was getting ready to run—she wasn't sure where she was going to go, maybe Kev's house?—the figure stepped out from the shadow of the trees, limping slightly.

George.

She let go of the breath she'd been holding and ran towards him. "Oh, thank god it's you." She hugged him before he could react. "I thought it was some crazy stranger lurking in the trees to hurt me. What were you doing there? You scared me about half to death."

He gently untangled himself and pushed her away. "I was keeping an eye on you. It isn't just tourists you have to worry about. A storm's coming in. Come on. Let's get you inside and warmed up."

He led the way back to the house, careful not to get too close to her. Jackie bit her lip, wanting to ask why he was avoiding her but scared he'd run again if she did. Instead, she followed along silently as he led her into the living room, pointed to one of the kitchen stools, and brought her the big blanket that was normally out on the porch.

He moved to the kitchen, and finally looked at her from the safety of the other side of the counter. "Pick your poison. Hot chocolate, coffee, or tea?"

"How about hot chocolate and some of those mint schnapps I saw in the cupboard?"

He grinned. "Can do."

She watched as he moved around the kitchen, filling the kettle and setting out two cups with a dash of schnapps and a heaping scoop of hot chocolate mix each. He was stiff as he moved, wincing slightly as he reached for each item, but she didn't offer to help, sensing somehow that this was his way of healing the rift between them.

"Your injuries still bother you?" she asked instead.

He nodded as he waited for the water to heat. "Especially in weather like this. I feel it in about five places now when a storm's coming in." He stretched his neck to each side and shrugged his shoulders.

"I guess that could be a handy skill if you're out on the water and an unexpected storm hits."

He grinned. "Yeah. I guess so. Every sailor should have at least one good injury he can rely on when radar goes down."

She desperately wanted to ask him about the night before, but the water finished heating and he turned his attention to pouring it into the cups and stirring them.

He pushed hers across the counter. "Careful, it's hot."

She blew on it for a second before taking a small sip. The warmth of the cup against her hands and the liquid as it made its way down her throat was just what she'd needed. She shivered slightly as it took hold. "It's delicious. Thank you."

She took another sip, watching him carefully. He still wasn't looking at her, but he'd made himself a cup, too, and hadn't fled back to his room, so that was something.

"So…" she asked as the silence stretched between them. "How was Auckland?"

"Good. I stayed with an old friend. I think you know her. Linda?"

Jackie almost choked on her next sip. "Linda? Pretty brunette, about five-two. Likes to do body shots."

George laughed. "Yeah, that's the one. She always was a fun girl."

"That she was." Jackie set her cup down. "So you're good friends, huh? Stayed the night and all."

"Yeah." He frowned at her. "Why? You have a problem with that?"

She did. But she shouldn't. It wasn't her business if he was hanging around with a drunk slut.

The nastiness of her thoughts surprised her and she frowned at the counter.

"Jackie? You okay? What's wrong?"

She fought to control herself as tears suddenly gathered behind her eyes. What was her problem?

She shook it away. "She, um…After Dave and I were really together—not during that five years of off and on bullshit—but about a year after that, she tried to hit on him. Well, not tried. She definitely did. I'd had to go back home for my sister's wedding and he'd stayed on in Miami and they were all out one night and she suggested they do some body shots with tequila. You know how bad Dave was at handling tequila."

George nodded. "So did he do them?"

"No. Thankfully. But I've never forgotten that she tried that."

"Do you think she really knew you guys were still together? I mean, to be fair, you had left him behind a few times before that..."

She took another sip of her cocoa, glaring at him over the rim. "She knew."

"When you did leave him behind it's not like Dave lived the life of a monk waiting for you to come back, you know."

"Glad she's such a close friend you feel the need to defend her and insult my husband at the same time."

George's eyebrows went up. "Jackie."

"Well."

"You were pretty wild yourself back in the day. And not always concerned with someone's relationship status. If some guy was there alone, you thought he was fair game."

She glared at him. "This isn't about me. And I've changed."

"Yeah, well, so has Linda."

"Has she?"

He nodded.

"So you guys, what, played Scrabble last night and then went to sleep in separate beds?"

He downed the rest of his hot chocolate and put the cup in the sink, shaking his head as he turned back to her. "Linda's married, Jackie. She has a two-year-old kid now and a great husband named Luke. We had fish and chips at the little dive around the corner and were all in bed by nine. Them in their bed, me on the couch. Satisfied now?"

She was too embarrassed to meet his eyes, so she just nodded.

As he stomped down the hall, leaving her alone at the counter, she buried her face in her hands. She'd really screwed it up this time.

What the hell was wrong with her? Why did she even care where he'd stayed the night or who he'd been with? He was a grown adult. He could do what he wanted. And shouldn't she be happy for him if he was feeling good enough to move on?

But she hadn't. She'd been...jealous.

CHAPTER 35

The next few days were tense as George did everything in his power to avoid her. He was up before dawn, gone to work on the boat or out kayaking or who knew what else. And at night he either disappeared into the garage to work on some project or another or said he had to go to a friend's and took off again almost as soon as he'd set foot inside.

Melody and Aidan tried to make the best of it, but they all knew the happy times they'd had those first few weeks were over.

And even though Jackie listened to hear George out on the porch each night, he never came.

Finally, after five days of bullshit, she'd had enough.

She waited up in the darkened living room until he stumbled home at one in the morning. He swayed slightly as he carefully opened and closed the front door, moving with the overly careful movements of someone who'd had one too many drinks and didn't want to trip or slam into something and wake everyone up.

As he moved towards the hallway, she called his name softly.

He froze, staring around with wide eyes like he'd heard a ghost. It was almost comical except for the fact that he'd been being such an ass the last few days. Finally, he spotted her.

"Jackie? What are you doing up?" He made his careful way towards her, bracing himself against the back of the other couch.

"We need to talk. Come on." She moved towards the porch, but he stayed where he was. "George? I said come on."

"We can talk here."

"No, we can't. I don't want Aidan and Melody to hear us. Come on. You could use the fresh air, too. Sober you up a bit."

His expression turned mulish, but he followed her outside anyway. She thought about going to the porch swing, but it was a beautiful night and she needed to move, the feelings whirling around in her gut were too much for her to handle sitting still. Plus, she hadn't forgotten that Melody had said she could sometimes hear them laughing from her room.

"Can you make it down the steps without breaking your neck or do you need my help?" she asked, voice clipped.

"I'm fine." He moved to the opposite side of the steps and carefully walked down each one, hand braced on the railing.

She didn't say anything—although she wanted to—as she patiently waited for him to join her.

Neither one of them spoke as they made their way to the beach.

Finally, when she was sure they were far enough from the house, she turned on him. "Do you want me to leave? Because if you do, I will."

"What? No. Who said that?"

"No one had to say it but when you can't even be in your own home because you're so busy avoiding me, it seems one or the other of us needs to leave and since it's your house...Unless you want to sell it to me?"

He shook his head. "No. I don't want you to leave. And I'm not selling you my house. Don't be ridiculous. I've just been busy the last few days, that's all."

"Bullshit. You're avoiding me."

He crossed his arms and glared at her. "Fine. I am avoiding you. So what? That doesn't mean I want you to leave. You've been doing so well here. I wouldn't take that away from you."

"But you are taking it away from me."

"What are you talking about?"

"Don't you get it? Part of the reason I've been doing so well is because of you, you lug." She poked him in the chest. "I mean, sure, New Zealand is gorgeous and all the walks I've been taking with Melody and all the delicious food Aidan has been feeding me have helped, but so has talking with you..."

"You can talk to Kev. Seems he had a good time that night at the pub."

"No, I can't. Not the way I can talk to you. You get it, George. He doesn't. And neither do Melody or Aidan." She stared up at him, pleading for him to understand, but he had his arms crossed across his chest and he wouldn't look at her.

"Please look at me. If you aren't speaking to me anymore...I can't." She bit her lip, tears forming in her eyes. "I can't lose you, too. Don't take this from me. Please." The tears started to fall, big drops that raced down her cheeks and fell to the sand.

"Don't cry. Oh no, don't."

But she couldn't help herself. She'd already lost Dave and nothing and no one could replace him, but George had helped fill a little of that emptiness with his warm, steady presence and now he'd pulled away from her and she was losing him, too, and...

George pulled her close, trembling as she buried her face against his chest. She tried to stop herself, but she couldn't. Sobs racked her body as he cradled her close, murmuring over and over for her to please not cry, that he'd never meant to hurt her, that of course he was there for her.

Finally, her tears ran their course and she pulled away from him, wiping her face on the sleeve of her sweatshirt, too embarrassed to look at him.

"Sorry," she mumbled. "I didn't mean to cry all over you like that."

He gripped both of her shoulders and forced her to meet his eyes. "Don't apologize. And I'm sorry if I added to your pain. I just..." He shrugged. "Are we okay now?"

"I don't know. Are **we** okay? Because I'm still not sleeping well at night and I really, really miss having you to talk to. And you can't abandon me to the lovebirds like this. Do you know what it's like to be the third wheel with those two?"

He laughed. "I'm sorry. That was very inconsiderate of me. I won't do it again."

"So we're good?"

"We're good."

They walked back to the house in silence, George's arm thrown around her shoulder and Jackie leaning against him for warmth and support. It felt good to have him back.

She needed him. And she suspected he needed her just as much.

CHAPTER 36

They carefully eased back into their former routine, George and Aidan working the boats and Melody and Jackie hiking and taking photos by day, all four gathering at the end of the day for dinner and conversation, and George and Jackie ending the night with their midnight conversations on the porch.

Late one morning as she and Melody hiked a local trail that ran between moss-covered trees with weird white bumps that looked like half a seashell sticking out of them, Melody finally asked, "So…George seems to be back to his old self?"

"Mmhm. He is. I think he just needed a little break from us for a few days. So, any idea what you guys will do after the season ends? Where are you headed next?"

Melody turned to look at her and Jackie tensed, hoping Melody would take the hint and let her change the subject. Because whatever existed between her and George was a fragile thing that felt like it could break at any moment and she didn't want to look at it too closely.

Melody half-shrugged and sighed, turning back to the path. "I'd love to stay on here, but Aidan says there just isn't enough demand during the off-season and neither one of us have enough saved to make it through. I mean, George would let us stay on for free, but...I'd hate to take advantage like that."

As Melody batted at yet another spider web blocking their path, Jackie silently wondered whether the spiders were ultrafast at building their webs or whether it had really been that long since anyone else had walked down this particular path. If the latter, it was a shame. She liked the trail. It wound down to a stream crossing and then back up another hill until it ultimately led to a gorgeous view out over the ocean and a perfect picnic spot.

Too bad most tourists who came to the area only went to one of two or three spots. Hot Water Beach and Cathedral Cove being the two main ones.

Well, at least it left plenty of trails for her and Melody to explore in peace.

"It might actually be good for George to have you guys stay on, you know."

"Yeah, maybe. But Aidan isn't one to sit idle for that many months."

"True. I'm sure he'd much rather be off earning good money sailing the Mediterranean or some other high-demand location."

They reached the top of the trail and walked across a meadow until they could see the ocean spread out before them. It was a perfect day. Not too hot, not too cold, the sky clear and blue unlike half the days when rain seemed to be threatening the horizon.

They spread a tarp and blanket on the ground and sat down to eat their lunch of tuna fish salad and crackers accompanied by Melody's homemade cranberry white chocolate macadamia nut cookies which were so delicious Jackie had already had five before they left the house.

Melody poked at her food before finally setting it aside. "Jackie?"

"Yeah?"

"Can I talk to you about something?"

"Of course." Jackie stared at her, surprised she felt she had to ask. "What is it?"

Melody bit her lip. "I want to have a baby."

"Oh." Jackie blinked, unsure what to say or do. Part of her wanted to smile and encourage Melody and say how wonderful that was, but a wave of bitterness crept up her throat and hovered behind her eyes. "A baby?"

"I know. What am I thinking when Aidan and I are so unsettled and money's tight and I don't even know if I can after the cancer treatment. I mean, what if I'm permanently damaged now?"

Jackie's concern for her friend won out over the bitterness and she reached out to squeeze Melody's arm. "You can't think that way. You have to be positive. I know there are women who've had cancer and then gone on to have perfectly healthy kids. I mean, I don't know what their situations were, but

I'm sure it's worth talking to your doctor to see."

Melody nodded. "You're right. Of course. That's the first step. Asking my doctor if it's even possible."

"Have you mentioned it to Aidan yet?"

She shook her head. "No…I…It's never come up. I mean, other than a 'you better get on something so we don't have any sort of accident' sort of thing." She grimaced. "You know him better than I do, do you think he'd want kids?"

Jackie frowned, thinking back over the years to the few comments Aidan had made about kids or parenting. Nothing he'd said indicated it was something he'd want or consider. More the opposite, actually. But she didn't want to dash Melody's hopes.

And people changed. If body-shot Linda could be a mother, Aidan could be a father.

"That's something you'd have to ask him about."

"Which means, no."

"I didn't say that. He's changed so much since he met you, I honestly don't know how he feels about it now. When a guy's young and having fun traveling the world being single, he'll say one thing, but when he gets older and starts to confront his own mortality, all of that can change. Dave didn't want kids when I first met him, but..." She choked on the words, swallowing back the sudden urge to cry.

"Oh, god, Jackie, I'm so sorry. I didn't mean to bring something like that up. I didn't know."

"It's fine. It's fine. Calm down. I'd rather you talked to me about these things than hid them from me, you know? If I'm really going to move forward with my life I have to start having these conversations. I mean, what kind of friend would I be if you felt you could never talk to me about half your life anymore?"

"Yeah. True. I just...Sorry." She picked at the edge of the blanket. "Maybe I should see if it's even possible before I bring it up with Aidan. No point having that conversation if it isn't."

"There are other ways to have kids. You could use a surrogate. Or adopt."

Melody blushed. "I never thought I'd be the girl saying something like this, but I really want it all. To be pregnant and have a kid that's a combination of him and me. I don't want to raise just any kid with him. I want to raise **our** kid. To see him or her grow up and think, 'Oh, I bet that's just like Aidan was at that age.' You know?"

"Yeah, I know." She'd imagined saying things like that when she'd dreamed of having a kid with Dave. Seeing a little mini-Dave running around, fishing pole in hand, talking about boats…

She shook away the thought. "So, call your doctor first. Maybe go in for some tests and see if it's possible. And then bring it up with Aidan if it is."

"I wonder how mad he'll be if he finds out I've been looking into it without discussing it with him first?"

"Oh, I don't think it'll be an issue. He loves you. Why would he get upset about that?"

Melody shrugged away the question, but she still looked nervous. Jackie squeezed her arm. "It'll be okay. Trust me. Aidan adores you."

"I hope you're right."

"I am."

CHAPTER 37

That night as she and George sat together on the porch swing, she told him what Melody had said about maybe wanting to have a child. She didn't think Melody would see it as a betrayal and she knew George would understand how much it hurt to have her friend considering a dream she'd decided could never be hers.

After she told him, he stared out at the night, rocking the swing slowly for a few heartbeats. Finally, he licked his lips and shifted to study her. "So you think you'll never have kids? You're still young, you never know what might happen."

She shook her head at the thought of carrying someone else's child. "I can't imagine it. I mean, I know people find other loves. You see it happen all the time. But…" She shrugged. "Maybe in ten years or so I could see that happening? But not now. Not anytime soon. Certainly not in enough time for me to have a child."

He nodded, his brow furrowed. "Sometimes I feel like that. Like no one could possibly compare to my Nellie. No one will ever be as beautiful or as fierce and amazing as she was. But other times…"

Jackie leaned forward, her eyes fixed on his face as his gaze went distant.

"Other times I think the worst thing I could do is deny what she gave me."

"What do you mean by that?"

He shrugged and continued to stare over her shoulder, not looking at her. "She showed me how amazing it is to share your life with someone you love. It took some doing on her part—there were a few rough edges she had to sand down—but she got me in shape to care and be cared for. And it would be a disservice to her memory to throw that away." He shook himself like a wet dog and turned to look out towards the beach again. "Listen to me, sounding like a complete sap."

He glanced back at her. "You're sure you don't want kids anymore? Because I have to say, I think you'd make a damned fine mother."

She bowed her head, fighting the tears that suddenly appeared in her eyes.

"What? What did I say?"

She shook her head, because she knew if she spoke those tears would fall.

"Jackie." He rested his warm hand on hers. "What is it? I didn't mean to upset you. Look at me. What did I say?" He lifted her chin with his fingers, searching her eyes.

"It's nothing. I just..." She inhaled through her teeth, the pain in her chest almost too much to bear. "Dave used to say that to me. We'd be lying there in bed and he'd rest his hand against my belly and stare into my eyes and ask if I was ready for kids yet, because he knew I'd be a fantastic mom."

She wiped at the tears on her cheeks. "He was ready long before I was. I'd actually..." She swallowed hard, fighting the tears. "I'd actually just decided it was time before he went on that damned trip. We were going to start trying when he got back."

She couldn't hold the tears back any longer, they overwhelmed her. George drew her into his arms and cradled her against his chest as she cried her heart out.

After she'd stopped, she thought about moving back to her side of the swing, but it was so comfortable there, sheltered in his arms, that she stayed.

She fell asleep, still snuggled against his chest.

CHAPTER 38

Jackie jerked awake, pulling away from George, body tense with panic. It was still dark but much later than when she'd fallen asleep.

"What time is it?" she demanded as he stretched his arm over his head. An arm that had to have been pinned in place the whole time she slept.

"It was three last time I checked my phone."

"You poor thing. You were stuck here this whole time unable to move or go to bed. I'm so sorry."

He shook his head. "Don't be. It was fine. You know I usually stay out here a lot later than you do." He shrugged, not quite looking at her.

She nodded, emotions she wasn't willing to acknowledge surging just below the surface.

"Well." He stood and stretched. "Now that you're awake, I best go get some real sleep."

"Wait." She stood, not sure exactly what she was doing. "We're still okay, aren't we? I mean…You're not gonna disappear and start acting funny on me again, are you?"

He laughed softly. "No. I'm not going to disappear on you."

"Promise?"

"Promise."

"Okay then." She hesitated a moment longer, not wanting to walk away from him and spend the rest of the night cold and alone. She bit her lip, wondering if she should ask him to come with her. Not for anything physical, just to share that comfort, to not be alone.

But he turned away before she could muster the courage. "Goodnight, Jackie," he called softly.

"Goodnight."

She stood there after he closed the door to his room, wanting to go after him. To ask him…

What?

To hold her?

To not let her spend another night alone?

But she didn't. He'd joked with her about breaking Kev and she'd laughed it off. But she wondered if something like that would break George. If he'd want or need more and if she'd be able to give it or if she'd run like she'd run from Dave so many years ago.

She couldn't risk it. Couldn't chance hurting him like that. He mattered too much to her.

She turned and went to her own room, pulling the cold sheets up to her chin, and trying not to think about how empty the rest of the bed was and how nice it would've been to have him next to her, his strong arms wrapped around her.

CHAPTER 39

As soon as Jackie made it to the kitchen the next morning, Melody accosted her. "There you are! What's up with people being slowpokes this morning? First George, now you. Did you forget today is our spa day?"

Jackie stared at her blankly for a moment before she remembered. "Oh, right. Massages and swimming and lunch."

"Uh-uh. And our massage appointments are at ten, so if we're going to get in a bit of a soak beforehand, we need to get moving. Now. Go get your gear, Missy."

"But...coffee."

"You can bring it with. I'll pour some into a carrier."

"And food."

"Aidan picked up some croissants for breakfast. You can eat one in the car. Go." She turned Jackie around and pushed her towards her room.

Jackie walked down the hall, still in a daze.

The massage was fine. It took place in a big airy room with plenty of sunlight. Jackie preferred her massages in calm, quiet, semi-dark rooms so she could drift to sleep. Instead the masseuse chatted to her the whole time about her Christmas plans. She was from Sweden and going home for the first time in five years.

At least she didn't ask Jackie much more than how long she was in New Zealand for and how she was enjoying it.

At the end, the masseuse asked about putting oil in her hair, but Jackie had been forewarned by Melody and politely declined. She didn't need oil dripping down her face for the next few days.

She and Melody met up in the dining room and both ordered incredibly yummy looking salmon salads. For a moment it felt like Jackie was back in California, just having lunch with a friend like before.

B.D.D. Before Dave's Death.

She poked at that thought. Other than the time she'd spent with Dave, did she miss that life? Shopping in San Francisco, having a fancy lunch somewhere, coming up with design ideas that were just unique enough to satisfy her clients but not so unique that they wouldn't fit in with their friends?

No. She didn't.

She'd liked living in Tahoe because she could share it with Dave. And her design business because it gave her something to do with her days. But without Dave to share it with...

No. If she never went back, she wouldn't care, wouldn't miss it at all.

"Do you realize Christmas is only two weeks away?" she asked Melody.

"Hard to believe, isn't it? When every single day here gets more and more gorgeous. I've never been somewhere summery for Christmas before."

"I know. Me neither. I always flew home no matter where I was. To my sister's most years. Except last year when she and her kids had to come to me because I didn't want to go anywhere and then it was horrible because I wouldn't let them decorate and I hadn't bought any gifts and..." She dropped her fork, hands fluttering in panic.

"What? What is it?"

"I haven't bought them anything. It's only two weeks until Christmas and I haven't even thought of getting them gifts."

Melody laughed. "It's alright. That's what online shopping is for. We'll go home, you can get online, order a bunch of stuff, and have it shipped straight to them. It'll easily arrive in time."

"Are you sure?"

"Positive. It's what I did for my dad and his latest young thing." She rolled her eyes. "You think he'd finally start dating women his own age one of these days, but they just keep getting younger and younger every year. I don't get it."

Jackie picked her fork back up and poked at her salad. "I might."

"What?"

"I might understand what he's doing. He doesn't stay with any of them that long, does he? They're just beautiful women he gets to sleep with and travel with for a bit, right?"

"Exactly." Melody shuddered.

"So no risk of losing someone the way he lost your mom."

"He didn't lose my mom, he left her."

Jackie stared Melody down. "Come on, now. You know that's not fair. He left because he couldn't handle her cancer coming back, but that doesn't mean he didn't lose her. It just means he wasn't strong enough to stay with her to the end. So not only did he lose her, he learned that he wasn't as strong a man as he'd probably thought he was before that happened."

Melody pressed her lips together and jabbed at her salad as if she was trying to kill it.

Jackie knew better than to push the conversation further, so instead she said, "I fell asleep in George's arms last night."

She knew she should probably keep it to herself, but she desperately wanted to understand what she was feeling and thinking and she suspected the only way she'd know is by talking it out with someone else. Also, she was worried she was hurting George somehow and she didn't want to.

Melody leaned forward, all of her attention focused on Jackie. "What happened?"

Jackie licked her lips, her mouth suddenly dry. "We were out on the porch, talking. Like I told you we do. And...I don't know. I got upset about something." She couldn't tell Melody about what—her friend didn't need to know how much it hurt to think about Melody and Aidan having kids. "And I started crying. And he held me. And then, he just kept holding me and I drifted off to sleep."

"Okay, that seems reasonable. Is that all that happened? Was he weird about it after?"

"No. Not really. I don't think. I made him promise he wasn't going to be weird about it."

"Oh, well, if you made him promise."

"I know. Sounds ridiculous." She picked up her fork and poked at her salad. "But he did. And then we just stood there for a moment. Like neither one of us knew what to do. And..."

"What?"

She bit her lip. "I kind of wanted to ask him to come back to my room with me. Not to have sex. It'd be simple if that's all this was about. But to...to hold me."

The waiter brought their glasses of wine and neither spoke as they tasted and gave their nods of approval. Only when he was out of earshot did Melody continue. "Why?"

"What?"

"Why did you want that? Are you falling for him?"

"No! We're just friends. I just...I'm tired of sleeping alone. Of being lonely. And I thought it would be nice to have someone there and that he'd understand."

Melody frowned at her. "Let me ask you something. Do you think that an attractive man and an attractive woman who are both single can be friends? And only friends?"

"Yes, of course. I've had lots of men who were friends of mine before."

"I didn't say men and women, I said an **attractive** man and an **attractive** woman. Who are both available."

"What's the difference?"

Melody raised her eyebrows and stared Jackie down. "Everything."

"How so?" Jackie knew she was being deliberately difficult, but she didn't care. She didn't like where these questions were going.

"Because if one or the other isn't attractive, then chances are nothing will happen. Because for something to happen there has to be mutual attraction there, right? But when both are attractive? And there's nothing else keeping them apart? I figure given long enough something will happen."

"That's ridiculous."

"Is it?"

"Yes."

"So you think you could sleep in the same bed with George, wrapped in his arms, his hard body pressed against yours, and nothing would happen?"

"Well, when you put it like that..."

"Exactly." Melody leaned forward. "I know this is a hard time for you right now, but...Do me a favor?"

"What?" Jackie snapped.

"Don't ask George to do that."

"Why not? Don't you think he feels the same way? Don't you think he's lonely, too?"

Melody bit her lip. "I think…I think George would…"

"What?"

"I think he'd think it was more than sleeping in someone's arms."

"But he isn't looking for anything right now. He lost Nellie less than a year ago. He's as emotionally hollowed out as I am."

Melody frowned at her, but didn't respond right away. Finally, she sat back. "Just…If you need something like that, maybe look elsewhere, okay?"

"Like where?"

"Oh, I don't know. Anywhere, really, if all you want is someone to share your bed. Did you see that guy at the pool this morning? The one in the blue swim shorts who was totally checking you out?"

"Was he? He was pretty good-looking. Although not as good-looking as the two guys we ran into on that hike the other day. The one in the khaki shorts? Yum."

"You noticed them? I didn't want to say anything, 'cause, you know."

"What does that mean?"

"Well, when you first got here you were pretty torn up still and it seemed a little rude to be pointing out hot men to you when you were still grieving your husband."

"Nonsense. It's never rude to share the world's beauty."

Melody laughed even though they both knew Melody was right and that Jackie would not have appreciated a comment like that even a few weeks ago.

"Hm. Well, anyway. Cheers to you noticing hot men again so I can mention them to you and not feel bad about it." Melody grinned like she'd been given the best gift in the world.

Jackie laughed. "Cheers."

They clinked glasses.

"I think this calls for a celebratory dessert." Melody waved the waiter over and ordered the apple torte and chocolate cake. As he walked away, she nodded at him. "He's not bad...You could ask for his number before we go."

"No. Just because I'm noticing attractive men again doesn't mean I need to be set up with one, thank you very much."

"I wasn't setting you up, I was just…admiring the scenery and trying to live vicariously through you now that I'm an old settled down boring type." She grinned a wicked little grin and Jackie couldn't help but laugh.

The conversation drifted to what Jackie might buy her nieces and nephews for Christmas, but in the back of her mind Jackie was still thinking about George and moving on and what she was going to do.

CHAPTER 40

Jackie paced her bedroom, trying not to chew on her thumbnail as she waited to hear the sound of George sitting down on the porch swing. Everything had seemed normal tonight—they'd all eaten dinner together, laughing and talking about the crazy group of Russian tourists George and Aidan had taken out earlier in the day.

But what if it wasn't? What if he didn't show tonight? What would she do?

She needed him. She'd come to rely on him to help her face each day. No matter how bad it got, she knew he'd be there at the end of it, a steady presence to listen and comfort her.

She couldn't lose that. Especially to something stupid like falling asleep in his arms.

She heard a creak from the porch and relief flooded through her. He was out there, waiting for her.

She rushed to join him, but he wasn't sitting on the swing. He leaned against the railing instead, looking out towards the ocean.

"George." She stepped closer, searching his face for signs of what he was thinking, but he was locked down, inscrutable.

"Jackie." He turned to look at her, his jaw set, the scar on his cheek stark in the moonlight that slashed across his face.

He was going to tell her he couldn't do this anymore, that something had changed last night and that he needed to walk away from this, whatever it was.

She couldn't let that happen.

"Wait. Don't." She stepped closer. "I'm sorry. About last night. I should've never put you in that position."

She reached for his hand. "You have been such a source of support for me since I've been here. And I'm sorry if I crossed a line and made you feel uncomfortable. I just..."

Before he could answer, she rushed on. "Your friendship has been like a lifeline to me these past weeks and I don't want to lose it. Please." She felt tears building behind her eyes. "It's just...I miss Dave so much sometimes...And there's this part of me that desperately wants what I had with him back..."

His hand clutched hers tighter. She continued, "But I know I can never find something like that again. And I'd be foolish to try." He pulled his hand free of hers and stepped away. "But I'm so glad I have this with you. That I can talk to you and know you get it, that you understand."

She reached for his hand once more, but he stepped away. "Say you're still my friend, please. Say we can still have our talks."

"Of course." The words were clipped and toneless. He wouldn't look at her.

She stepped closer, but he stepped back, keeping his distance.

She bit her lip, watching him. "Did you want to sit down?"

"How about a walk on the beach instead? It's the perfect night for it."

"Okay."

She didn't want to walk on the beach, she wanted to sit next to him on the swing and feel it vibrate as he laughed that deep, rich laugh of his. But if that's all he could offer right now, then she'd have to accept it.

She followed him down the steps and out to the beach. It was a gorgeous night. Warm and clear and full of summer. They walked side-by-side, not touching, chatting about their days and the gifts Jackie had picked out for her family back home.

She watched George carefully as they talked. He seemed fine. But there was a niggling voice in the back of her mind reminding her that George was good at hiding his real emotions behind laughter and jokes. That the more at ease he seemed, the more outgoing and gregarious, the more he had a wall up to hide from the world.

To hide from her.

But why? What was he hiding?

CHAPTER 41

Jackie and George eased back into their old routine of ending the days with late night talks, but something had changed. They no longer sat on the porch in the cozy intimacy of the dark sharing their hurts and concerns. On clear nights George insisted they walk the beach, just once to the end, and then he retreated to his own room, leaving her alone far too soon. On rainy nights he leaned against the porch railing or the wall of the house or didn't come out at all.

Jackie blamed herself for the change. She'd asked too much of him and he didn't have it in him to tell her no, so he made sure it could never happen again. He'd pulled back, no longer talking about Nellie at all.

She watched in silence, longing to comfort him, but not wanting to upset him. She knew how grief could ebb and flow, pulling you back under when you thought you'd finally found your way past it. He'd talk about it again when he was ready. And she'd be there for him when that time came.

In the meantime she continued to improve, gaining strength and color and weight as she and Melody hiked every day and they ate Aidan's delicious cooking every night.

Christmas came and went without much fanfare. They didn't even put up a tree or any sort of decorations other than the stack of gift-wrapped presents from their families that they'd piled in the corner.

The actual day was sunny and ninety degrees (Fahrenheit—she still hadn't adjusted to thinking about temperatures in terms of Celsius), nothing like the snow-covered Christmases back home.

They'd agreed not to exchange gifts but they went out kayaking together in the afternoon and grilled steaks and vegetables on the barbecue and entertained themselves opening Christmas crackers and wearing the silly paper crowns around for the rest of the evening.

The next day—when it was actually Christmas in the States—Jackie Skyped with her family, glad she'd remembered to order them something before it was too late, even though she suspected from her niece's reaction that the clothes she'd ordered her weren't what girls that age were actually wearing these days.

The most entertaining part of the holiday was watching Melody try to hide her reaction when she opened the gift her father had sent her while talking to him live on Skype. It was a set of edible body paints in various flavors of chocolate. Jackie, who was sitting out of sight on the other couch at the time, could clearly hear Melody's father explain how he and his latest girlfriend had enjoyed playing with their set followed by the girlfriend's giggle and "Shhh, you're not supposed to say anything about that" in a voice that made her sound about ten.

Melody turned beet red, smiled extremely hard, and mumbled thanks while Aidan laughed so hard he fell off his chair. She ended the call as soon as she could and they all had fun teasing her the rest of the day about when she was going to put the body paints to use.

It was a good week.

And a good month.

By New Year's Eve, Jackie felt ready to take that next step, to find someone who'd help remind her what it was like to just live in her body and enjoy the moment for a few hours instead of constantly be weighed down by her emotions.

And she had the perfect person in mind. Kev. They'd crossed paths a few more times since that night at the bar and he'd always been just as flirtatious as before, letting her know that if she was ever interested, he certainly was, too.

Even better, he and his housemates were hosting the neighborhood New Year's party.

So she had an interested man, an opportunity to see him, and George's endorsement that he wasn't such a bad sort of guy. (Not that she'd mentioned her plans to George, but she remembered what he'd said that first night about trusting Kev with his sister.)

C.K. Carr

Now all she had to do was actually go through with it.

CHAPTER 42

Jackie leaned close to the mirror, applying bright red lipstick with a practiced flourish. It looked great against her sun-tanned skin and went perfectly with the stunning red dress she'd ordered online the week before.

She smiled at her reflection, noting how her cheeks had filled back in and her hair was once more shiny and luxurious although a little more sun-streaked than it had been in years. She needed to start wearing a cap when she hiked or she'd regret when the wrinkles came.

But for now she was just happy to finally be back to looking like she had before. There were a few new fine lines around her eyes and mouth—not all of them from smiling—but that was to be expected. Just like a person didn't stay the same on the inside as they aged, they shouldn't stay the same on the outside either.

And tonight she was going to dance and laugh and kiss a man.

She shivered with anticipation.

It had been too long.

But she was ready. Ready to take that next step and move forward.

She smoothed the dress along her hips—curvy again, thankfully—and shook her hair out one last time before making her way to the living room where the others were waiting.

Aidan let out a low whistle as he pointedly looked her up and down. "Hot damn, Jackie. Who do you think we're going to see tonight? The King of England?"

She shrugged his tease away as Melody jumped to her defense. "Give her a break, Aidan. Sometimes a woman just wants to look pretty. And you definitely do." She grabbed Jackie's arm and leaned closer to whisper, "This for anyone in particular or you just putting it out there to see what you attract?"

Jackie grinned. "There might be a certain guy I have my eye on."

Melody hunched her shoulders in delight but then smoothed her expression and stepped away, looking far too innocent as Aidan narrowed his eyes at her.

George was sitting on the couch, engrossed in a fishing magazine.

"You ready, George?" she asked, wanting him to say something about how she looked.

"Yep." He threw the magazine on the couch and stood but still didn't look at her.

Aidan opened the door. "Come on, kids. Let's go bring in a new year and hope it's better than the last one."

"That won't be hard," Jackie muttered, still watching George out of the corner of her eye, but he stared ahead, completely ignoring her.

CHAPTER 43

Jackie saw Kev the minute she stepped through the front door. He made a beeline for them and drew her close, dancing with her for a moment to the music blaring from speakers in the living room. "Jackie, my love. So glad you're here," he whispered, his breath hot against her neck.

Jackie shivered with anticipation as his hand slid down her back. "Me, too," she murmured.

"You look amazingly gorgeous tonight," he purred, stepping back to admire her.

"Thank you."

"Of course, you're always beautiful, don't get me wrong." He stepped closer again, stroking the side of her face with one finger.

246

"Hey, Kev, can I get a hand?" Aidan interrupted.

"Can't it wait?"

"No. That faucet that's always giving you problems. Looks like someone messed it up again."

"Find Mark, he'll fix it."

"Why would I do that when you're right here?"

Kev glared at him. "Let it go. It's not that bad of a leak."

"Oh, I don't know about that. Remember that one time in Sydney, how bad things got?"

Kev dropped Jackie's hand like it had suddenly burned him. "Yeah. Lead the way."

Aidan disappeared into the galley-style kitchen and Kev started after him.

"Wait. You'll find me later won't you?" Jackie asked, searching his face for that spark of desire that had been there just a moment before.

"Um, yeah. Of course." But his words were flat and he didn't look back at her as he left.

"Come on. Let's get a beer," Melody grabbed her wrist and dragged her out to the back patio where a big cooler sat, stuffed to the brim with bottles.

As Melody handed her a beer, Jackie glanced around. "Where's George?"

"Must've gone around back when we arrived. Of course, I was too busy watching you and Kev. So that's your target for the night or were you just warming up?"

Jackie laughed, but she didn't have a chance to answer, because a couple of guys approached and she found herself bantering back and forth with them. And when they moved on, a couple others replaced them, and then a couple others and then a couple others.

She enjoyed the flirting, but she didn't let any one man get too close, just kept it light and fun. It was wonderful—that feeling of being desirable and wanted. Of being alive.

She drank a little, but not too much, knowing it was best to keep her wits about her. Occasionally, she looked for George, but she never saw any sign of him.

Aidan finally returned and pulled Melody away to dance, but Kev never did. She caught glimpses of him from across the room, but he never drew close enough for her to get his attention. She was never alone, though, she always had at least one admirer keeping her company, and often more than one.

As the hours ticked towards midnight she found herself watching Melody and Aidan. They danced slowly no matter what the music was, ignoring everyone else as they stared deep into one another's eyes and murmured back and forth. Jackie laughed, watching them, because no matter the song Aidan just did the same little two-stepped shuffle back and forth.

It didn't matter. The love between them shone like a beacon—in the way they touched and looked at one another, the way they were so effortlessly in synch. Jackie trembled, wondering if she'd ever be able to find something like that again.

What if Dave had been her one chance? Not at happiness—there were plenty of men in the world who'd make her laugh and who she'd enjoy spending time with—but at that sort of soul-deep love that was stronger than anything; that bond that could see two people through any challenge.

She turned away, unable to watch them anymore.

Where was Kev? She needed to forget herself for a little bit. To lose herself in the touch of a hand on her hip and lips against her neck.

She saw him by the cooler, putting new bottles into the melting ice, and excused herself from her current batch of admirers. She could've just picked one of them, but she wanted someone she knew and trusted. Or at least someone the men she trusted trusted.

"Hey, Kev," she said, leaning against the railing. "You abandoned me back there."

"Oh, Jackie. Hey. Well, I guess I underestimated the amount of time needed to host the party properly. If you'll excuse me...Better go check on things."

He backed away from her, his former flirtatiousness gone.

"Oh no you don't." She grabbed his arm and pulled him into the shadows. "What's wrong? Why the one-eighty?"

"What are you talking about?"

She glared at him. "You've been flirting with me for weeks. You even flirted with me when I arrived. Or don't you remember running your hand down my back and whispering in my ear?"

He glanced towards the party once more. "I really need to get inside. I'm sorry, Jackie. I am."

He pulled free and ducked back into the party.

CHAPTER 44

Jackie watched Kev go, too stunned to move. What had just happened? Why had this man who'd been flirting with her for weeks, who'd clearly wanted her, turned so cold so suddenly?

She looked away, fighting the tears that threatened to overwhelm her. Why did this have to be so fucking hard?

She wanted Dave back. She wanted life to be simple again. To be with a man she loved and who loved her, to be dancing with him in the middle of the room, oblivious to everyone else around them because she was so madly in love she didn't care about anything but him.

A hand touched her back and she flinched. Probably one of her damned admirers. She turned to glare at

252

whoever it was and tell them to get away, but it was Aidan, with Melody hovering behind him, looking concerned.

She wiped the tears away. "What? What do you want?"

"You okay?"

"No."

"Why? What happened?" He looked around, ready to hurt whoever had made her cry.

She backed further away from the party, not wanting anyone to see her like this. Aidan and Melody followed.

"I thought Kev liked me. You saw how he was when we arrived. But then…Just now…" She clutched her arms tight across her chest. "He practically ran away from me. Why? What's wrong with me? Why doesn't he want me anymore?"

Melody stroked her arm. "He was probably just busy, that's all. There's not a straight man here tonight that doesn't want you. You're gorgeous."

Jackie couldn't keep the tears back any longer. She sobbed and turned away.

"Oh, honey. Don't cry." Melody pulled her into a hug.

"This is all so hard. I hate it. Can we just go home now? Where's George?"

"I haven't seen him at all. Aidan? Have you seen him?"

Aidan shook his head. "I think he left."

"Left? When? And why would he leave before midnight?"

Aidan didn't answer. Jackie wiped at her face and nose. She probably looked like a hot mess now, with mascara running down her cheeks and red swollen eyes. No one would want her looking like this. Or if they did, they'd be some creep trying to take advantage. The night was ruined.

Kev was across the room leaning close and flirting with some blonde. "Look at that. Look at him flirting with her. I thought you guys said he was a good guy."

"He is," Aidan said, his words short and clipped.

Melody shook her head. "No he isn't. Look at that. It's not right to flirt and lead Jackie on like that for weeks, and then snub her like he did and turn around and be all over some chick ten minutes later." She set her drink down.

"I'm going to have a little word with him."

"No, you're not." Aidan moved to block her.

"He needs to explain himself."

"Melody, let it go. You've had a bit too much to drink. You still want to yell at him in the morning, you can. But not right now."

"Aidan, I love you, but get the hell out of my way. Now."

Aidan clenched his jaw as he looked down at her. "It isn't Kev's fault."

"How do you figure that?"

Aidan exhaled through his nose as he glared back and forth between them. "Come here. Both of you." He led them to the far end of the porch to a spot that was almost quiet before continuing. "I'm sorry, Jackie. The reason Kev went cold on you is because of me."

"You told him about Dave dying? Why? He didn't need to know that." Jackie moved deeper into the shadows, feeling vulnerable and exposed, like everyone knew she was a poor grieving widow.

"No. That's not what happened."

Melody glared at him. "Then what did you say? And why?"

Aidan clenched his jaw again, looking back and forth between them. "I..." He shook his head, clearly not wanting to tell them.

"Well?" Melody tapped her foot on the ground. "We're waiting."

Jackie wanted her to stop. It didn't matter, none of it did, the night was already ruined, but she just slouched against the wall and watched Aidan search for words.

He sighed. "I told him that if he was a real friend, he wouldn't be that guy."

"What guy?" Melody asked.

"The guy who goes after the girl his buddy is in love with."

Jackie and Melody stared at him, confused, and then looked at each other. Who...

"George?" Melody asked, a slight smile on her face.

Aidan nodded.

Jackie scoffed. "No. George isn't in love with me. We're just friends. Ask him. He'll tell you."

Aidan looked at her for a long moment. "Jackie...I love you, but sometimes you're a fool when it comes to men. He left the minute Kev pulled you close. And I saw his face before he turned away. He may not even know what he's feeling, but he does love you."

"And you just let him go? Aidan!"

"He was fine. And I'm sure he didn't want me to make a big deal out of it. He just couldn't be here watching you guys all night."

"But...If I'd known..." She looked around, suddenly frantic. "I need to go. I need to see if he's okay."

"Alright. We'll walk you home."

"No. Stay. If he's there I want to talk to him alone."

And she was going to need those few minutes to figure out what **she** was feeling. All the time they'd spent together, all the secrets they'd shared, the way they'd been there for each other day in and day out since she'd arrived...

She'd told herself it was just friendship.

But maybe...

Maybe it was more than that.

She had to see him. She had to know.

C.K. Carr

Was he really in love with her?

CHAPTER 45

Jackie rushed down the street, wondering what she was going to say.

She didn't want to ruin this, but how did you go from friends as close as they'd become to something more? In all of her relationships, sex had come first and emotion second. She didn't know how to move from emotion to sex.

It wasn't that George wasn't attractive to her. Even with his scar and limp he was still one of the best-looking men she'd ever met. The scar actually leant him a certain air of tragedy that was immensely appealing. If he'd been a stranger, she would've easily and happily slept with him.

But...

He'd become so important to her. Her rock, her strength, her anchor in the storm of her grief. Her hands shook at the thought of ruining what they had by trying to make it more.

She couldn't lose him, couldn't lose what he'd given her.

She shivered, thinking what her life would be like without him in it. Dark. Empty. Lonely.

She didn't want that. She'd rather be celibate the rest of her life than lose him.

But if she did have a chance to be with him—to take what they had and make it that much better—she had to try.

She just hoped Aidan was right. Because if he wasn't...

This was going to be a disaster.

CHAPTER 46

As soon as Jackie saw the driveway, she knew George wasn't there. The house was dark and cold and his car was gone.

She could barely breathe as she opened the door, wondering where he'd gone and if he was alright. This was the first time he'd driven since Nellie died. And it was dark and there were probably a bunch of drunken fools out. And who knew what kind of state his mind was in right now.

He'd left a note on the kitchen table. It didn't say much, just that he'd decided to go over to Nellie's folks' house and wouldn't be back for a few days and not to worry.

She tried to call his cell, but he'd left it behind. She could hear it ringing from his bedroom.

She hung up and stared at the note again. How much was he hurting right now? He thought she was with Kev. He didn't know that nothing had happened. Or that...

That she loved him.

She hadn't thought it was possible, but she did. Why hadn't he told her what he was feeling? They could've avoided so much heartache if he had.

But then she remembered all those times she'd talked about how she wasn't ready for love, that she couldn't imagine ever finding something like she'd had with Dave. All the times she'd mentioned finding someone to sleep with, but refused to even consider finding someone to love.

What had she been thinking?

Why had she missed what was right there in front of her? Such a great, amazing man had wanted her and she hadn't even known. How was that possible?

Then again, she'd never had to wonder if a man liked her before. Most men were like Kev or those guys at the party, flattering her, fawning on her, letting her know exactly how much they were interested.

Oh, George.

She collapsed onto the couch, thinking back to when they were younger and wondering...

Had he liked her even then? He'd always been there with a joke and a smile. And she'd certainly found him attractive. But she'd always assumed that if he were interested, he'd let her know. Maybe he'd assumed the same.

That was the problem when you took two people used to having the other person make the first move. They didn't know what to do when it was their turn.

She turned on the television, needing the noise to distract her from her go-nowhere thoughts.

It was almost midnight.

She sat alone in the living room, watching the hosts countdown from ten, the people in the crowd shouting and cheering and kissing as a new year dawned, and wished George were there with her.

She didn't know when she'd crossed that line from friendship to love— probably around the night she slept in his arms—but she had. And now all she wanted was to tell him how she felt.

It was a new year. Time for a new start.

CHAPTER 47

Jackie thought about emailing George the next morning, but what she had to say was best said in person.

What if Aidan had been wrong and George hadn't left because he saw her with Kev but because a New Year's party was just too stark a reminder of Nellie and all he'd lost? Maybe that's all it was.

Maybe she was alone in her suddenly awakened feelings.

And if that was the case, an email from her confessing her feelings wouldn't go over well. He might never come back if he saw that.

She tried to distract herself by focusing instead on Aidan and Melody. Something had happened that night after she'd left. They were tense, not looking at each other, sitting at opposite ends of the breakfast bar, focused on their laptops or talking to her but not each other.

It didn't help that a rainstorm came through early on the first and didn't leave, trapping them inside together. No hikes, no boat trips. Just three tense and angry people stuck in a house that suddenly felt far too small.

On the second day, Jackie begged Aidan to call George and make sure he was okay. He frowned at her over his laptop. "He's a grown man, Jackie. He's fine."

"But it's the anniversary of Nellie's death today. And what he thinks he saw...If he feels the way you said he does..."

He turned his attention back to his computer. "You women, always trying to meddle with something that's just fine the way it is. He'll be back in a couple days. If he wanted us to reach him, he would've taken his phone. He didn't. Let it go."

She turned to see Melody glaring daggers at Aidan. What was up between them? Whatever it was, it needed to end. This was ridiculous.

"Melody. Can I see you in my room?" She didn't wait to see if Melody responded or followed before marching down the hall and sitting cross-legged on her bed.

It took a minute, but Melody finally showed up. She didn't come in, though. Instead she leaned against the doorframe. "What is it?"

"What the hell's wrong with you and Aidan?"

Melody glanced down the hallway and then stepped into the room, closing the door behind her. Jackie patted the spot next to her and Melody sat down, but didn't speak, studying her hands instead.

"What happened?"

"I…" Melody shook her head, her voice quavering with unshed tears. "On New Year's Eve, after we'd come back and were lying there in bed, I…I brought up having a kid with Aidan."

"And?"

"And he said absolutely not. He literally sat up and moved away from me like I had some sort of disease he might catch."

"Did he tell you why?"

She nodded, a tear making its slow way down her cheek. "He said he was too selfish to be a father. That he didn't want to make the sacrifices it would require. That he liked his life the way it was."

"Oh, honey, I'm sorry." Jackie squeezed her shoulder. "But surely you guys can work through this, can't you?"

Melody shook her head, the tears falling faster.

"Melody..." She forced Melody to look at her. "Do you really want a child that bad? More than you want to be with him?"

"I don't know..." Melody sighed, squeezing her hands together. "I love him so much. And I've never been happier than I am with him. But..." She punched the mattress. "Why does it always have to be so hard with him? First, he stayed with Lynn all those years after we met and I never knew if we'd get here, because he wouldn't let her go to give us a chance even though I knew he was unhappy. And now this."

Melody closed her eyes. "All I wanted was to find a man I could love and grow old with. And, I never really thought about it much, but kids were part of that. I want to be eighty-years-old, on

Christmas Day, surrounded by my children and their children tearing open packages and running around out of control. I don't...I don't want to spend it sipping a beer on a sun-drenched porch somewhere alone or just with Aidan. I love him. But..."

"But you want more. What if you leave him and don't find it? Would you rather be alone than stay with him without children?"

Melody stood to pace the room.

"Melody?"

"I don't know. I mean...If I leave now there's a chance I'll find someone who does want kids. But if I stay...It'll be too late."

"But you love him! I saw it. The way you two danced together at the party. Don't you understand how rare what you two have is? You can't just go out and find that again. It's not that easy!" She realized she was shouting and that she'd stood as she spoke, her hands fisted at her sides. She turned away. "I'm sorry. I just...I'd give anything to have what you two have."

"I know. And...You're right. What I have with Aidan means so much to me. I don't want to lose it. But...Staying means letting go of a dream of my future that I never really realized I had. And I'm not sure I can do that."

"Maybe you need to talk to him again. Now. When you're both sober and after he's had some time to think about it. Maybe he'll change his mind."

"Have you ever known Aidan to change his mind?"

Jackie half-laughed. "No. But there's a first time for everything, isn't there? And if there's any person in this world who can make that happen, it's you."

Melody looked in the direction of the living room. "I don't want him to be the father of my children because he loves me. I want him to do it because he wants kids, too."

"Melody." She swallowed, fighting the pull of the memory. "Sit."

Melody sat down and Jackie told her about her and Dave. How he'd wanted kids pretty much from the day they got together, but how she just couldn't imagine being a mom yet, but how over time and over years she'd come to realize that having his child was something she truly did want.

"So, see? He might come around eventually. Like I did."

Melody's tears had dried up. She bit her lip as she watched Jackie.

"What?"

"When did you decide you wanted kids?"

Jackie pinched her nose to hold back the tears. "Right before he left for Malta with Aidan. We were going to start trying when he got home."

"Oh, Jackie."

Melody pulled her into a hug, and Jackie couldn't hold back the tears. She sobbed on her friend's shoulder for all she'd lost and for how scared she was to try again, to let herself hope that maybe she was being given a second chance with George.

It was too scary to think about.

She pushed Melody away. "Go. Talk to Aidan. And don't walk away from the amazing thing you have just because he's not there yet. Okay? Promise?"

Melody nodded. "Promise."

"Good. Now go. I'm going to take a shower and wash these damned tears away."

CHAPTER 48

By the time Jackie finished her shower, Melody and Aidan were nowhere to be seen. She assumed they were in their room, talking things through. Outside it was pouring down rain in huge, gusting sheets. She debated curling up on the couch and watching t.v., but her heart wasn't in it. Instead, she slunk back to her room, buried herself under the covers, and went to sleep, hoping George would be back soon and she could see whether Aidan was right or not.

The next morning it was still raining, but she found Melody and Aidan laughing and talking together while Aidan cooked enough food to feed twenty people. There were pancakes, eggs, fried potatoes, sausages, bacon, and a quiche.

She glanced towards the door to make sure George hadn't come home sometime after she'd fallen asleep, but she didn't see his car in the driveway.

She snagged a piece of bacon as she took her seat. "Um, Aidan, you do know there are only three of us here this morning, right?"

"I know. But I like to cook when I'm happy."

"So you two worked through things, then?"

Melody nodded. "Yeah. I took you advice and decided to give Aidan the time he needs to get comfortable with the idea of being a dad. I'm still going to look into what I need to do medically to make it happen, if anything, but otherwise we're going to put it aside for the time being."

Aidan slid a pancake from the skillet onto a stack that was already ten deep. "She's given me a year. Twelve months of coupled bliss. And then we'll see where we both stand."

"Good. I'm glad. What you two have is special. I'd hate to see you throw it away over your first argument."

Melody laughed. "Oh, that wasn't our first argument."

"Oh no." Aidan poured Jackie a cup of coffee and handed it to her. "That wasn't even our first argument since you've been here."

"Really? But I never heard you guys yelling at each other."

Melody blushed. "Yeah, that's probably because I prefer to write things down rather than talk them out. I've sent a few testy emails Aidan's way both before we were together and after."

"You have email fights?" Jackie couldn't believe they were serious.

"Yep. I dash off some angry upset message and then go off for a hike. Aidan gets a chance to read it while I'm not around, does whatever he needs to do before responding, and then sends me back a message about how he feels about it."

Jackie looked at him. "Are you serious?"

He nodded. "Works pretty well, really. No saying something cruel in the heat of the moment. Although I have learned by now that I need to check my email before I head home. There was that one time I didn't check and she'd sent me a really pissed off message and I came home thinking things were all fine and swell and got my ass handed to me."

"I did not hand your ass to you."

"No, you just shoved my phone into my hand and suggested I read it while you did something better with your life than sitting around waiting for me to get my shit together, and then stormed out of the house and slammed the door after you."

"Was that here?" Jackie asked.

"No. Brazil." Aidan's eyes were twinkling as he leaned across the counter and kissed Melody. "It might seem crazy to everyone else, but it's how we first came together, so it works for us. Right?"

"Right." Melody smiled at him, her face full of love.

Jackie had to look away from them, the thought of having a love that powerful too much for her to handle right then.

Aidan cleared his throat. "Come on, Jackie. Stop slacking. How many pancakes you want? Two? Three? Five?"

"One, thanks."

"Oh, come on, now. You can at least eat two." He threw two on a plate and shoved them her way.

She rolled her eyes, but took them, glad her friends had worked through their issue and were back to normal.

For now.

CHAPTER 49

That night, Jackie lay awake listening to the storm raging outside. Wind whipped at the window shutters and slammed tree limbs against the roof as the rain poured down, battering the house. She was going crazy, spending her nights alone, huddled in her bed wondering where George was and how he was doing, not knowing when he'd be back or how he felt.

She'd never been in this position before and she hated it.

A car door slammed, the sound barely audible over the roar of the storm. She sat up, wondering if it was one of their neighbors coming home late or...

No. She heard the front door slam closed. It had to be George.

She stood and stared at the door to the hallway. She wanted to go to him, to tell him nothing had happened with Kev, to see how he was, but something held her back.

For the first time in her life she didn't know what to say to a man.

Or do.

She was trembling like a child, scared as much as excited. She strained to hear the sound of his footsteps in the hall, or maybe his voice—although she was pretty sure Melody and Aidan had already gone to bed—but all she heard was the crash of the storm.

She stood there in silence, paralyzed, waiting, wondering, straining to hear him, knowing she needed to talk to him now, tonight, before it was too late and she lost her courage. But she couldn't bring herself to move.

She heard the distinctive creak of the board on the porch and turned to stare in that direction even though she couldn't see anything.

What was he thinking going outside in this mess? He'd get drenched.

As if to prove her point, a gust of wind threw rain against the door, shaking it in its hinges. She didn't want to go out in that mess, she wanted to stay inside where it was nice and warm and dry. But George was out there, possibly upset and hurting, thinking he'd lost her and remembering how he'd lost Nellie.

She had to go to him.

She wrapped her blanket around her shoulders and opened the door. A gust of wind tore the door out of her hands and she wrestled it closed behind her, not wanting her room to get soaked. She squinted in the direction of the swing but George wasn't there.

Just as she was about to turn around and go back inside, feeling foolish, she saw him, leaning against the railing, staring towards the ocean, arms braced as if challenging the storm to do its best. A gust of wind and rain swept across the porch and she staggered under the assault, but he stood firm.

She was already soaked through—the blanket hadn't helped at all—her clothes clinging to her body, her hair plastered to her face. At least it wasn't cold. It was almost refreshing.

Almost.

She threw the blanket on the swing and pressed forward, moving to

C.K. Carr

George's side. "What are you doing out here?" she shouted in his ear.

He was drenched. The t-shirt and shorts he was wearing so wet they clung to every curve of his muscular chest and thighs. She found it hard to breathe, staring at him, wanting him—wanting to run her hands along his muscular chest and arms, to press her body close to his. But she couldn't move, couldn't bring herself to close that last bit of distance between them. Not without knowing how he felt.

He grinned at her, but didn't respond.

"George! You're soaked to the bone. What are you doing out here?"

He laughed. "Enjoying the storm. Aren't you?"

"You're enjoying this?" she demanded as another gust of wind and rain swept across the porch.

"Of course. What's not to love? Raging wind, torrential rain. It's nature at her finest. Don't tell me you've never just stood in the midst of a storm like this and let it pour over you?"

"Uh, no, can't say I have."

"Come on. Let me show you." He held out his hand, his eyes alight with excitement.

280

Something Gained

She reached out, a thrill coursing through her as their hands touched. His smile was wild and free as he led her down the steps and into the heart of the storm, the wind whipping at their bodies, the rain so heavy it even got into her eyes.

In the middle of the back yard, he let go of her hand, threw his arms wide and laughed with joy, spinning in a circle as the storm crashed around them.

Jackie stared at him, mesmerized. She'd been so worried about him and here he was, dancing in the rain, smiling like he didn't have a care in the world.

He lowered his arms and finally looked at her. His eyes ran up and down her body, the hunger of his gaze like a physical touch.

She stared at him, suddenly unable to breath, waiting, hoping. She stepped forward, reaching for him, hoping he'd reach back. That she wasn't alone in how she felt.

For a heartbeat, he watched her, his hands by his side.

And then he stepped forward and wrapped her in his strong, powerful arms, his mouth taking hers as the storm poured down around them.

CHAPTER 50

Jackie lost herself in the sensations of kissing him. The entire world disappeared as their mouths and bodies met, their hands stroking water-slicked skin, their tongues tasting and exploring.

Somehow they managed to pull their soaking wet shirts off so they stood skin-to-skin in the midst of the deluge, water pouring down upon them, tracing every curve of their bodies. They were hungry, ravenous for something so long denied and so desperately needed.

They touched and kissed as the storm raged around them, oblivious to anything and everything except one another.

Eventually, George took her hand and led her back towards the porch. She resisted for a moment, not wanting to move from the spot where she'd finally found what she hadn't even known she'd been missing, but the hunger in his gaze drew her onward.

He stopped at the top of the stairs and pressed her against the railing, exploring her body with mouth and hands and tongue, driving her to heights she hadn't touched in what felt like forever. She gasped and writhed under his hands, riding wave after wave of pleasure, completely lost in the moment.

And then it was her turn to explore his body. To trace the lines of muscles and scars as she kissed and touched and tasted and drove him to the edge over and over again until it was finally too much and they stumbled to her room, wet bodies tangled together, collapsing onto the bed, losing themselves in the feel of one another, in the waves of lust and longing that washed through their bodies as they finally came together.

It was unlike anything she'd ever experienced. Every touch was like fire on her skin. Every kiss reached some hidden part of her she'd never known existed.

They spent the rest of the night reclaiming the pieces of themselves they'd lost to grief and loneliness until at last the storm ended and they lay next to one another, sated.

Jackie fell asleep with her head pillowed on his shoulder knowing she was exactly where she should be and with exactly the man she should be with.

It should've felt awkward—two people who'd never been together before and with so much pain behind them—but it wasn't.

It was…perfect.

CHAPTER 51

Jackie stretched, eyes still closed, luxuriating in the afterglow of the night before and the feel of once more having a man stretched out by her side. And not just any man. George. A man she trusted implicitly, who'd taken her to levels of passion she hadn't even known were possible.

She shivered slightly and pulled away from him, her gaze immediately going to the nightstand where the photo of her and Dave sat.

She'd been so happy with him. And yet...

She'd never felt with him the way she did in George's arms.

She closed her eyes.

She'd break if she pursued that thought any further. Instead, she turned to look at the amazing man at her side, a smile curving her lips as she leaned in to kiss him softly, her body still glowing with memories of the night before.

George pulled away from her and sat up, turning so his back was to her.

"George? What's wrong?"

"Jackie...What happened last night...I'm sorry...I..."

"You're sorry? For what?"

He stood. "I shouldn't have...I knew you were looking for something simple and I...I have to go."

She moved to block his path, not caring that she was buck naked. Glad for it, actually. Let him see and remember how wonderful they'd been together. "What are you doing? Where are you going?"

He shook his head, not looking at her.

"George. You are not going to run from me again," she growled. "Not after last night. No. I'm not letting you do that."

She stepped closer and ran one hand along his muscular chest, her fingers tracing an eagle tattoo that was now cut by a jagged scar. She bit her lip, already wanting him again, her blood on fire with what she wanted to do with him.

"Don't." He stepped back so she couldn't touch him.

"What's wrong? Don't you remember how wonderful we were together? Don't you want to do that again? Just one more time?"

She reached for him and he stepped away again. "No. I can't be that for you, Jackie. I'm sorry."

"Can't be what for me?" She glared at him, furious that he'd made her feel the way he had and was now rejecting her.

He moved to the door to the hallway. "Your fling. Your rebound. Your..." He shook his head. "I can't do it." He opened the door.

Jackie lunged for him. "Wait! That's not..."

But he was already halfway down the hallway, and a clearly shocked Melody was staring back at her from the bathroom doorway. "What was that about?" she asked.

"Nothing." Jackie stared down the hallway, wanting to go after him and explain that she loved him and last night hadn't been just some little fling and that nothing had happened with Kev and…

Aidan stepped out of his room and gave her a once over. "Glad to see you're looking better than when you arrived, Jackie, but maybe you should put on some clothes?"

She blushed furiously and retreated to her room.

She tried to put on the yellow sundress she'd brought from home—it was the easiest thing to throw on—but it no longer fit. And by the time she'd grabbed a pair of shorts, a bra, and a t-shirt and made her way to the living room, George was gone.

Again.

CHAPTER 52

"Where did he go?" Jackie demanded when she found Aidan in the front room and saw that George's car wasn't there.

"Good morning to you, too, Jackie. Glad to see you managed to find some clothes."

"Shut up. Where is he?"

Aidan grinned at her. "Come on, now. Can't a guy have a little fun when he sees his housemate starkers in the hallway?"

"Not when she's just slept with his other housemate who didn't stick around long enough to find out that it really meant something to her and wasn't some sort of rebound fling." She threw herself down on the other couch. "Where is he?"

"I don't know. Didn't say anything to me. Just walked out the door, keys in hand."

"Do you guys have a tour today?"

"Yeah."

"Good, then I'll go with you when you head down there."

"No."

"Aidan! I need to talk to George. He doesn't know that nothing happened with Kev and he just thinks last night was some sexy rain-drenched hookup."

"Sexy rain-drenched hookup? Oh really?" He leered at her.

"Shut up. Just...I need to see George and explain."

"Save it for when he gets home. Today's a bunch of VIPs from a travel magazine. No way I'm letting you barge in there and ruin things for him."

"But don't you get it? He's upset. He thinks last night was something it wasn't."

"Sorry, Jackie. You're just gonna have to wait." He stood and walked away down the hall. She glared after him.

She couldn't wait. This was too important. She had to talk to him.

Now.

And then she realized. If it was such an important day, he was bound to have his phone with him. She could call him or at least text him.

But no sooner had she had the thought than Aidan returned. "By the way, I'm taking this with me today. It's for your own good." He waved her phone in the air.

"Give that back." She lunged for him, but he moved out of her way with practiced ease.

"Nope. Trust me. George will be just fine. And if it looks like he isn't, I'll step in and let him know that, what? Nothing happened with Kev? Anything else?"

She glared at him.

"Well?"

"And that last night wasn't a fling."

"No? What was it then?"

"Something I need to talk to **him** about."

Aidan laughed. "Ah, Jackie...You are certainly hard on men's hearts, let me tell you."

"I'm not trying to be. I was all prepared to tell George how I felt last night, but he was outside and it was so loud and he was so wet and…"

"No, no, no. I do not need to hear about that. Whatever rain-soaked romp you two had is between you." He stepped away from her. "Now I better get going before I'm late. You and Melody have fun today. And don't worry. I'll be there the whole time. Nothing's going to happen to George. And when he gets home, you two can go off and do whatever you're going to do and I'll be sure to wear some ear plugs so I don't have to hear it."

"Aidan!"

He ducked out the front door with a final wink, slamming it behind him.

CHAPTER 53

"Come on," Melody said a moment later. "Let's go for a drive. It's actually almost nice out and the forecast says no rain."

"Melody, I need to see George. I need to tell him what last night was really about."

"You heard Aidan. It's a big day for George. Whatever you have to say can wait."

Jackie glared at her. "I thought you were my friend."

"I am."

"So why are you both treating me like I'm some ten-year-old kid?"

Melody leaned against the counter. "Look. I don't know exactly what happened last night, and I'm not asking, but do you really want to have whatever conversation you want to have down at the dock when George is trying to prep for this important tour? With maybe Aidan and Kev and who knows who else around?"

"No. But…"

"It can wait. He'll be home tonight and then you guys can talk about it for as long as you want. Aidan and I'll even go out to dinner so you have the whole place to yourselves."

"What if he doesn't come home, though? What if he runs away again?"

"Then you call him, text him, email him, whatever it takes."

Jackie's eyes darted toward Melody's laptop.

"But first you try to have this conversation face-to-face. Give it ten hours, that's all we're saying."

"Fine." She didn't want to, but it did make sense.

And she did want to have this conversation in person. To tell George she loved him and see his eyes light up and the same love she felt shine back at her. And then to kiss him. Again and again and again.

She sighed. "So where are we going today?"

"Coromandel Town? It'll let us try somewhere new and get far enough away from here that we don't run into anyone we know. Plus, after the last few days of rain, I don't think either one of us are going to want to hike. Those trails'll be a muddy mess. Sound good?"

"Sure." Jackie didn't really want to go anywhere, but she knew she'd go crazy sitting around the house waiting for George to come home.

"Good. You gonna change first?"

Jackie glanced down. "What's wrong with what I'm wearing?"

"Your shirt's inside out, for starters. And I thought you said you were getting rid of those shorts because they're too small. I mean, they look okay, but..."

"No. You're right. I just threw on what came to hand." She shrugged. "Not sure why I was so worried about putting on clothes. I should've just chased after George and to hell with it."

"Well, **I** appreciate that you did, because naked people sort of freak me out. Although I should thank you for being the reason I got to see George in all **his** naked glory. That is one fine man you have there."

Jackie laughed. "Thanks?"

"You're welcome. Now. Go get ready. Let's get going."

CHAPTER 54

Jackie changed into a better pair of shorts, turned her shirt around, and threw her hair back in a ponytail. She debated putting on a bit of make-up in case they went somewhere nice and then realized she was in New Zealand and that, with very rare exceptions, no one was going to care what she was wearing or how she looked. Especially not in a small touristy town like Coromandel Town.

She resolved not to discuss the details of what had happened with George. That was between them and none of Melody's business, but her resolve only lasted as long as it took for them to drive to Coromandel Town and find a nice restaurant with an outdoor patio.

By then she'd been thinking about it for over an hour straight while Melody had chatted about anything and everything else—including the weather, fishing, the New Year's party, her father's latest travel plans, and how she wanted to order a new lens for her camera.

After their waiter left them alone with a nice bottle of Sauvignon Blanc from the Marlborough region, Jackie couldn't hold it in any longer. "George and I had sex last night," she burst out.

"Oh, is that what happened? I wasn't sure when I saw you both buck naked this morning." Melody winked at her.

"Oh, shut up."

"Well, you know, there could've been some other explanation. Like a game of late-night, naked Twister?"

Jackie laughed and relaxed just a bit more. She took a sip of her wine, not sure what to say next.

"So…?" Melody raised an eyebrow. "How was it?"

Jackie shook her head, not sure she was ready to go there yet.

"Okay, you don't want to talk about that. Then…**How** did it happen?"

Jackie studied the tourists walking up and down the street in front of the restaurant, trying to figure out how to explain it.

"Fine. We won't talk about that yet either. Let's see...Maybe you can tell me what that little scene was about this morning?"

Jackie studied her fingernails. She'd been chewing on them a lot lately. She needed to stop that.

"Bueller? Bueller? Do I need to remind you that you're the one that brought it up, not me?" Melody stared at her expectantly, but Jackie didn't know what to say, her emotions were so close to the surface she was afraid that if she started talking about it she might lose it.

Melody shrugged. "Fine. All I have to say is that man has a **damned** fine body. I had no idea. We may have to make him walk around naked more often."

Jackie laughed and, just like that, the flood gates burst, and she poured out the whole story from hearing George come home and wanting to go to him to tell him nothing had happened with Kev to realizing he was out in the rain and...

She stopped there, biting her lip, as Melody leaned forward, eyes wide with interest. "And then? Is this where it gets juicy?"

Jackie shook her head. "No. I mean. Yeah." She buried her face in her hands, looking around to make sure the waiter wasn't nearby. "It was…" She couldn't help but smile. "It was amazing. More…" She frowned. "More amazing than anyone I'd ever been with before."

Melody winced. "Even Dave?"

Jackie nodded, sitting back, her arms crossed across her chest. There. She'd said it. She'd admitted that what she'd felt with George was better than anything she'd ever felt with Dave—the supposed love of her life.

"You want to talk about it? If not, I understand."

Jackie swallowed, wondering if she did. She shuddered slightly as she poked at the thought, wondering if she could talk about it without crying.

"We don't have to. We can just talk about George's nice ass. And…other attributes. Although, admittedly, I only got a glimpse. You'll have to fill me in on that more yourself."

Jackie laughed. "No. It's okay, I think. I do want to talk about it." She fiddled with her fork and then set it aside with a sigh as she searched for the words. "When Dave and I got together for the first time, I was only twenty-two-years old. I was brash and crazy and young. Too young. He wasn't my first by any stretch of the imagination. But..."

Melody waited while she thought it through.

Fiddling with the fork once more, Jackie continued. "The type of sex I'd had before that was casual. It was fun. It didn't mean anything. Even those first few times with Dave were just for fun. I didn't expect anything to come of it. We didn't have some deep connection, we were just two people who were physically attracted to each other. I mean, sure, I felt something more stirring beneath the surface, but I wasn't looking for it."

She rubbed at her face. "Don't get me wrong. Dave was an amazing man. He was so good to me. He loved me unconditionally. And I loved spending time with him. He...adored me. And I adored him."

"That was obvious the few times I saw you two together."

Jackie barely heard the words. "He was a great man. And I would've happily spent the rest of my life with him. But he wasn't…gorgeous. Or…" She sighed. "That skilled a lover."

She rubbed the back of her neck as she winced at the admission. "He was good. Don't get me wrong. He just wasn't…amazing."

"And George was amazing?"

She shook her head, laughing softly. "I can't believe I'm telling you all this, but…I have to for you to understand."

"It's fine. Tell as little or as much as you want."

Jackie bit her lip, thinking back. "I don't want you to think the times I had with Dave weren't good, because they were. But even before last night he wasn't the best I'd been with. The sex isn't why I fell in love with him. I fell in love with him for his big heart and his booming laugh and the way he wanted so much out of life and treated me like I was the most precious thing on this planet."

"All good reasons in my book." Melody took a sip of wine, still watching her.

Jackie nodded, thinking it through as she spoke. "And they were. I was happy with Dave. But last night with George..." She smiled just remembering it, brushing her fingers against her lips. "I...We...We were sooo perfect together. It was like our bodies were made for one another. And..."

She started to chew on her thumbnail and then pulled her hand away from her mouth, sitting on her hand so she wouldn't do it again. "I was so much more relaxed than I'd ever been with anyone else. I mean, sex was never a big deal to me. I never put this emotional weight on it like some people do."

"Like me."

She laughed. "Yes, like you. But at the same time. Even though I didn't make a big deal out of it, I'd never..." She frowned, struggling to describe it. "Other than with Dave, after we were really together, I'd never brought a deep emotional connection to sex. I'd slept with friends, but I'd never slept with someone I'd opened to emotionally like I have with George. Sex was always just something physical I did for pleasure. Does that make sense?" She caught herself chewing on her thumbnail again and grimaced.

"Yeah, I think so. So with George, because of all those late-night porch conversations you had over the last couple months, you'd built a strong emotional connection with him?"

"Mmhm."

"And probably a level of trust you've rarely felt with anyone else?"

Jackie nodded.

"So when you guys had sex you were a hundred percent comfortable with him and trusted him completely, so were able to let go with him in a way you never had with anyone else?"

She nodded again.

"Maybe even Dave?"

Jackie sighed.

She wanted to deny it. But she couldn't.

She'd loved Dave with all of her heart. She'd wanted to spend her life with him and raise children with him and hadn't imagined herself being with anyone else. But because of how they'd started—with sex for sex's sake and not having those deep emotional conversations that she'd had with George over the last two months—it had been different.

She crossed her arms tight across her chest.

"You okay?"

"I loved Dave."

"Of course you did."

"I trusted him. He was my husband. I didn't keep anything back from him. We had a good marriage."

"I know. Everyone could see that."

"But..." She slammed her hand down on the table, making the glasses jump. Why was this so hard to say?

"But you somehow let George in deeper than you'd ever let Dave in. And you feel guilty about it."

Jackie nodded.

"Don't."

"What?"

"Don't. Look, George came into your life when you were a different person than the woman who loved Dave. Losing Dave broke you open in a way that you'd never been broken before. You were more vulnerable, more exposed than at probably any time in your life. Do you think anyone wants to put themselves out there that much, even with someone they love? No. It's not realistic to think that you would've done that before."

"So why did I do it now?"

"Because you couldn't help yourself. You were so damaged you couldn't protect that deep inner core that most of us never let someone else see. And I suspect the same was true of George. He let you in in a way he probably never had before, even with Nellie. It doesn't mean you guys didn't love them. It just means that what you have now is on a different level than you were capable of having then."

Jackie chewed her lip, wondering if that was true. And what it meant for them going forward. Would they come together because of how deep their bond was?

Or would one of them run, too scared by being that exposed to another person after knowing how much it hurt to lose someone you loved?

More specifically, would **she** run? Could she actually handle this?

She didn't want to hurt George, but...

She was scared by how intensely she felt about him after just one night.

CHAPTER 55

The drive back was pleasant but long. Thanks to the storm, they'd decided not to take the dirt road that would've let them shortcut the drive, so they wound their way through rolling green hills along the coastline.

Melody filled her in on her progress on the baby front. She'd made a phone appointment with her doctor back home and he'd assured her that she should be able to have a baby no problem. Well, no problem other than the fact that it would be considered a geriatric pregnancy.

They had a good laugh over that one. Who would've thought that a thirty-eight-year-old woman would be considered geriatric?

"Of course, Aidan still hasn't come around to the whole idea yet." Melody's fingers drummed nervously on the steering wheel.

"Give it time. He will. Just...Don't push it. The more you bring it up with him, the more he'll resist. He's contrary that way."

"So what am I supposed to do? Just sit back and pray? I'm not much of a believer in that kind of thing."

"No. Just make sure he realizes what an amazing life he has with you. He'll work out the rest of it."

Melody bit her lip, slowing the car as they came around a corner to find a logging truck ahead of them. "Problem is, at the same time I'm reminding him what an amazing life he has with me, I'm reminding myself of it, too."

"Yeah, that's the hard part. Do you want what you have with Aidan even though it may not be what you thought life would look like when you settled down? Or do you want to move on and risk never finding something as amazing as what you guys have, but at least you'll have the kids and family Christmases when you're eighty?"

"That's the problem, alright." She sighed. "And what makes it harder is that I don't really care about the baby and toddler and teenager stages. I don't necessarily want to be a mother responsible for raising a well-adjusted child. I just want a family when I'm older. If I could skip all the in-between—travel the world with Aidan and have a fun exciting life—and then suddenly have a happy family around me when I'm too old for the rest of it, that would be my ideal."

"You really don't want to hold a baby in your arms? Or be pregnant and feel a life growing inside you?"

"No." She shrugged. "I know. It makes me some sort of lesser person to not want that, but I really don't. And the thought of being some PTA mom sort of horrifies me."

"Melody!"

"It does." The logging truck pulled off the road onto a dirt track and Melody sped past him. "Maybe Aidan has it right. Maybe we're good the way we are and I should just enjoy every moment while I can. I'll probably be miserable as a mother."

"Oh, I doubt that."

"What about you? Do you want kids someday?" She winced as soon as the words were out of her mouth. "I'm sorry. I don't know what I was thinking. Ignore the question."

"No, it's fine. I...I think I do want kids. It took me a long time to reach that point, and for a while there, I thought maybe I only wanted kids if they could be Dave's, but...No. I think I do want kids still. Someday."

"With George?"

She laughed. "It's too early to think about that."

But even as she said the words she could imagine how gorgeous a little girl would be with his green eyes and her brown hair. She shook the thought away.

It was too early. They'd only just slept together. And George still didn't even know how she really felt. And she certainly didn't know how he felt. All she knew so far was that he refused to sleep with her again if it was just a fling.

That didn't mean he loved her and wanted to have children with her, though.

CHAPTER 56

Aidan and George weren't there when they returned home. Jackie glanced at the clock. It was already three o'clock. "How long was that tour supposed to be for?"

"I think it was a lunch cruise, so probably until two or so?"

"Then where are they?"

Melody shrugged. "I wouldn't worry about it. They probably went out for a beer afterwards. You know, schmooze the VIPs a bit like they both do so well."

Jackie frowned, upset that George wouldn't rush right home to see her. But, then again, why should he? He still thought the night before had been a disastrous fling that should've never happened.

As the hours ticked by, she grew more and more agitated. By five o'clock, she was going out of her mind. "Text Aidan. Ask him when they're going to be home. Ask him how George is."

"Jackie…"

"Do it."

As Melody reached for her phone, it started to ring. "See? There's Aidan now. I told you it was fine."

She answered the phone with a smile. "Hey Aidan, we were starting to wonder where you guys are. You know we can't cook for ourselves anymore, not after how you've spoiled us all summer."

There was a pause and Melody's face fell.

"What? When? Is he okay?"

Jackie reached for the phone. "What happened? Let me talk to him."

Melody held a hand out to stop her, listening intently. "Oh god. Okay, yeah. We'll meet you there. What's the address?" She reached for a pen and then stopped. "No, that's fine. I can look it up."

"Let me talk to him!" Jackie screamed, reaching for the phone again.

"Jackie wants to talk to you, okay? Okay, love you." Melody held the phone out to her.

Jackie stared at it like it was a poisonous snake, suddenly scared to hear what Aidan would say. Finally, she took the phone and held it to her ear. "Aidan? What happened?"

"Jackie." He sounded so serious. Just like he had the day he'd called to tell her Dave had died. She flashed back to that call and her body tensed with dread. "What happened? Is George okay?"

"He was..."

"Is he okay, Aidan?"

He sighed. "He's alive. And he'll recover. But he isn't okay. Might not be for a long while."

She stumbled to the couch and collapsed onto the cushions. "What happened?"

"He was crossing the street and stepped in front of some fool driver going too fast."

"Oh no. Can I talk to him? Please?"

"I'm sorry, Jackie. He's in surgery right now. Car hit his bad leg and the damage is pretty extensive. And they're worried about a brain injury. They said they'll probably keep him in a coma for a bit to make sure he's okay."

"Did you tell him, Aidan? Did you tell him that I love him?"

He was silent on the other end of the line, and she knew he hadn't.

And now she might never get the chance. She was going to lose George just like she'd lost Dave.

Before she could throw the phone across the room, Melody pried it out of her fingers. "We'll be there soon," she said and hung up.

"I should've told him. I should've gone to the dock this morning. Or told him last night the moment I saw him. I should've let him know." She sobbed, all the fear that she might lose George and memory of losing Dave, crashing down around her and drowning her.

Melody held her as she cried, murmuring over and over again. "He'll be okay, Jackie. And when he comes out of the coma you can tell him exactly how you feel. It's going to be okay. It is. This isn't like with Dave. He's just hurt. That's all it is. It'll be okay."

But all Jackie wanted to do was run as far away as she could and hide from everyone and everything. She couldn't go through this. Not again

CHAPTER 57

Jackie didn't remember any of the drive to the hospital. She knew Melody was there, talking to her, assuring her it would be fine, that George was in good care and stabilized now, and Aidan was with him, and to just keep calm. But all she could think was how losing George would hurt too much to bear.

She couldn't handle this. She couldn't.

All her life she'd been so strong. She'd made it through her mother's death. She'd traveled the world and set her own path, never stopped, never for one moment worried what might go wrong, just charged ahead, knowing every experience was part of the adventure.

But that was before she'd lost Dave.

C.K. Carr

And now George...

She couldn't do it. She couldn't keep it together anymore.

She needed George to pull her close and tell her it was going to be fine, that he was there for her and that he loved her and that together they could make it through anything. But he was in a coma and might never come out of it. Might be permanently damaged.

Might not remember the amazing night they'd spent together...

This couldn't be happening. But it was.

Melody took control when they arrived, asking about George at the reception desk and leading the way to the waiting room where Aidan stood, looking out a window, his jaw set, every line of his body tense.

She'd forgotten until that moment that he'd been there when Dave died. That he hadn't been able to save him and now here he was waiting to find out if another friend was going to pull through. Dave had been like a father to him. And George was one of his best friends.

She wasn't the only one hurting right now.

Something Gained

"Aidan," Melody ran to him.

He held his hands out to stop her before she could hug him.

He was covered in blood. George's blood.

So much of it...

"Did you bring me a change of clothes?" he asked and Melody nodded.

Jackie stared at him. The blood was dark and crusted now, but at some point just a few hours before it had flowed, bright and red, from George's body. She stumbled backward. She couldn't do this. She couldn't.

Aidan caught her arm. "It's okay, Jackie. It looks worse than it is." He took the clothes from Melody, never releasing his grip. "Come on, Jackie. Why don't you sit down? Melody will stay with you while I change and then I'll let you know the latest. Okay?"

She couldn't speak, her mind too busy imagining the horror of George lying in the middle of the street, his leg shattered, bleeding all over the pavement.

She let herself be led to a chair and sat down, numb, unable to move or think.

She stayed like that until Aidan returned, now wearing a clean t-shirt and slacks.

She stood. "I can't do this. I can't...I can't lose George, too." She couldn't focus, couldn't look at Aidan or anything else.

"You're not going to lose him, Jackie. He's stable. Doctors say he's going to pull through just fine."

She shook her head, all the secret fears she'd been carrying around for the past year crashing in on her. "But don't you see? He was just crossing the street and this happened. What about...? What if next time...?" She buried her face in her hands, knowing that even if George was fine today he might not be tomorrow. One bad storm, one bad heart, one bad luck moment and she'd be all alone again.

Aidan shook her. "Jackie, look at me."

She didn't want to, but she did.

"That's life. You can never know what tomorrow is going to bring. Never. I wake up every morning and wonder if Melody's cancer might come back one day. Don't you think she does, too? Or that she worries about me when I'm caught out in a bad storm? But you don't walk away from love because of that. You don't say no to today just because tomorrow might be the end of things." He stared deep into her eyes. "Instead, you grab it like there's no tomorrow and you hold on tight. As tight as you possibly can. And you just pray to get as many good days as you can out of it before the end comes."

She bit her lip, still wanting desperately to run.

"Those five years you had with Dave. Were they good years?"

"Yes."

"Would you have rather lived them alone? Or with whatever random man took your fancy on any given night?"

"No." She pulled away from him, crossing her arms across her chest. "But that was different. I didn't know."

"So now you do. Now you know it doesn't always end happily ever after. That doesn't mean you don't try again. It just means you savor every moment you have that much more."

She bit her lip.

"Don't lose what you have because of fear, Jackie."

She didn't want to. But she didn't know if she could do this. Every cell in her body was screaming at her to run before she lost him. Before she had to go through that darkness again. Because she knew she wouldn't survive it this time.

Not without George.

CHAPTER 58

She would've gone insane during the four hours they waited to see George if it hadn't been for Melody and Aidan. They never left her alone. One was always at her side, talking, laughing, keeping her distracted from thoughts that wanted to spiral into that black place she'd lived in after Dave died.

The ugly thoughts kept surfacing, though, during those small lulls in the conversation.

Would George still be able to walk? And to work?

What kind of rehab would he need?

Was there any brain damage? Would he be a different man now?

What if he'd forgotten all those nights they'd spent talking? Or last night?

C.K. Carr

Her mind spiraled around every bad possibility until she was almost sick.

Finally, they led her back to his room, Aidan on one side, Melody on the other. It would've never been allowed in the States, but fortunately it was here. They understood that friends were sometimes more close than family and that for a tourist traveling in a foreign country a friend might be the only familiar face.

George lay in a big hospital bed, eyes closed, head bandaged, face bruised and cut, a tube down his throat, the machine by the side of the bed swishing with each movement of his chest.

Jackie didn't have words. She stood in the doorway and stared at him, all the fears of the last four hours racing through her mind. She'd always been so strong, so in control of every situation, but she couldn't move, couldn't speak.

Fortunately, Melody took control, drilling the doctor with so many questions the guy probably thought he was on trial. But he answered each one calmly, explaining that George was going to be kept under for a bit longer so they could monitor his progress and that he should be fine.

The only major issue was his leg. The same one he'd injured before. Lots of rehab ahead, but he shouldn't lose it.

Jackie breathed a sigh of relief when she heard that. She loved George for who he was on the inside, but she knew that a man couldn't suffer an injury like that and not change in some way. Especially a man as fiercely independent and adventurous as George was.

Aidan nudged her forward. "We'll be right outside if you need us," he said, and then he, Melody, and the doctor left her alone with George.

She moved to the side of his bed and took his hand, the tears flowing down her cheeks. She squeezed his hand, careful not to touch the needle embedded in the back. "You better not have been distracted because of me, you fool man."

She stared at him for a long moment. Even with the scar on his face he was still gorgeous, his strength showing in every line of his face. He was her rock, the foundation she wanted to build her new life on.

C.K. Carr

She leaned close. "Listen to me, George Killian. If you hadn't left so suddenly this morning, I would've had a chance to tell you how I feel. To let you know what really happened on New Year's. But since you had to be a damned fool, I'm stuck here talking to you in a hospital room and you probably can't hear a damned thing I'm saying. But just in case you can...

"I love you, George. I wasn't expecting this. I'm not even sure I want this. But I do. With all of me, with all of my heart, and all of my soul. And that's so hard to admit, because I loved Dave, too. I would've happily spent the rest of my life with him, but that's not how it worked out. And I don't know why I'm telling you this, but I think you'll understand. That I love you, but it's hard to admit it. To let go of what I felt for Dave and acknowledge what I feel for you."

She wiped at the tears on her cheeks. "You better pull out of this. Because I can't do this again. I can't lose another man I love. Do you hear me? You pull through or I'm gonna...I'm gonna hurt you." She laughed at the ridiculousness of what she'd just said.

"I love you, you foolish, stubborn man." She kissed his cheek. "And I just hope you love me, too. I hope Aidan was right about that. Because if he wasn't…" She let out a deep breath. "I'll still love you. It'll just…hurt. A lot."

She started to leave and then turned back. "And nothing happened with Kev. It shouldn't matter. Even if it had it would've only been physical. But I want you to know that. Now get better so we can start a new life, would you?"

Aidan and Melody were waiting for her down the hall.

"Ready?" Aidan asked.

"I don't want to leave him alone."

"Jackie. He's not gonna wake up for at least another day. You need to go home, rest, and gather your strength so you can be there for him when he does wake and in the days after that. They're not going to be easy."

She didn't want to, but she let Aidan lead her away.

CHAPTER 59

Jackie didn't sleep at all that night. Alone in her room all the fears overwhelmed her.

She could leave now...Get out before she was in too deep.

They'd only had one night together. It wasn't that serious yet. If she left now, maybe she wouldn't be hurt. Not as much as if he died some day in the future.

She'd lose him, yes, but on her own terms, not fate's. She'd know that she'd walked away instead of having him ripped from her when she least expected it.

No random call on some sunny day to tell her she was going to be alone again.

She could leave now, before she'd built her world around him.

She refused to picture how wonderful a life with George would be. Or to acknowledge how awful one without him would be. Instead she focused on how hard it would be to lose him if she stayed.

She had to go.

She had to run.

Now.

It was three in the morning when she logged onto her computer and bought a plane ticket from Auckland to San Francisco. She didn't know where she'd go when she landed. She couldn't go home.

But she couldn't stay here a moment longer.

She couldn't do it. She just couldn't.

No.

She tried to call a cab, but they weren't willing to drive her all the way to Auckland. Instead, she took the keys to Melody's car and left a note. "Sorry. Had to go. I'll leave the car in long-term parking at the Auckland airport."

She wanted to say more. To tell George she loved him, but she was too numb to find the words and too scared that if she started to write them out she'd change her mind and stay instead.

By four in the morning she was on the road, with no company but her twisted and dark thoughts.

As the sun rose on the horizon, her phone rang for the first time. It was Melody.

She ignored it.

Aidan tried next.

She ignored him, too.

She knew they'd tell her this was crazy and try to convince her to come back; give her all the reasons she couldn't just leave the man she loved in a coma in a hospital room in New Zealand.

But she didn't want to hear it.

Her fear drove her forward. She couldn't stop to listen to any other voice, not even the one screaming in her mind that this was wrong, that she needed to turn around and go back to George now, before it was too late. Before he woke up and saw that she wasn't there and heard that she'd left him behind in his darkest moment.

She drove onward.

CHAPTER 60

Unfortunately for Jackie, the only flight she could get was that night. She found herself at the Auckland airport with ten hours to spare. Even access to the Koru Club lounge wasn't enough to entertain her for ten hours although it did allow her to take a nice hot shower and get a massage.

But she still had eight hours left when that was all done. She sat in the hammock chair in the corner and tried to sleep. Relaxed at last, the black panic that had driven her all night finally receded enough to let her really think about what she was doing.

She was running.

Plain and simple.

She was scared as hell by how much she loved George so she was running away from him. Just like she'd run from Dave all those years.

And even if George chased her the way Dave had—which she wasn't sure he'd do, even knowing that Dave had eventually succeeded—it wouldn't change the fact that she was still the same woman she'd been at twenty-two.

A woman who was too scared to acknowledge how deeply she loved a man.

She'd wasted five years running from Dave. Five years they could've had together. Who knew how different things might've been if she'd stayed that first time?

Maybe they'd have two kids by now who looked just like him. Maybe he'd even be alive today, because he would've listened when she told him to go to the doctor for a check-up. Or he would've eaten differently or exercised more or...

She shook her head. Down that path lay insanity.

But the core truth remained. She'd lost five years she could've had with Dave because she was too scared to stay and love him.

And here she was, doing the same damned thing with George.

What was she thinking?

She pulled out her phone and called Aidan.

"Jackie. Where are you? Are you okay?"

"Didn't you get my note?"

"Yeah. But…Are you really at the airport? You were really gonna just fly home and leave George here?"

"I was. But I'm not now. I changed my mind. If he wakes up before I get there, tell him I'm on my way. Okay?"

"Where do you want me to tell him you are in the meantime?"

"Tell him the truth, I don't care. But you damned well better emphasize that I'm coming back for him and there's nothing he can do to shake me off. I love him too much to walk away, whether he wants me there or not."

"Oh, he'll want you there, no doubt about it."

"Good."

"Drive safe."

"Thanks."

She took her duffle—still her only piece of luggage—and headed for the doors feeling better than she had in weeks.

She was going back to be with the man she loved and she wasn't going to let anything stand between them from here on out. Not her doubts, not his injuries. Nothing.

They belonged together. And she was going to see that it happened, whatever it took.

CHAPTER 61

The whole drive back, Jackie worried that George would wake up before she got there and realize she'd run and jump to all of the wrong conclusions. And she was tired, too, now that the adrenaline driving her to run had drained away.

But she had to get back to him. She had to tell him what she felt. To his face. When he was actually awake.

She drove straight to the hospital. Melody was there, waiting for her. "Jackie. Oh, I'm so glad to see you're okay."

"What are you talking about?"

"You do know it's not normal to steal someone's car and leave in the middle of the night to flee the country, right?"

C.K. Carr

Jackie opened and closed her mouth, not sure what to say. "Well, there wasn't a cab to take."

Melody laughed. "Okay, well that makes it all alright, I guess. Glad you're back. Come on."

She felt the urge to turn and run again but fought it down. "Is he already awake?"

"Yeah. But, don't worry. You didn't miss anything." Melody started to walk her down the hall towards his room. "They had to take out his breathing tube, which I assure you you didn't want to be here for. And that was maybe an hour ago and the doctors have been checking him out since. So, really, you have perfect timing."

They stopped outside the room. Aidan came out to meet them. "He's waiting for you."

She was more nervous than she'd ever felt before. She didn't know why. This was just George. She'd known him forever. But...

It was hard to be vulnerable like this. To put yourself out there and tell someone you loved them when you weren't sure they felt the same.

336

But she had to. She couldn't lose him. Not now. And she couldn't accept this being less than it could be. He'd been an amazing friend and source of support these past months, but she'd seen how much more they could be that night they'd spent together and she wanted that, too.

More than anything.

She stepped into the room, forcing a smile. "Hey there. Heard you decided to get run over by a car," she teased, twisting her hands together.

"Yeah. Well. I figured things weren't exciting enough that day, I had to spice it up somehow." His smile was more of a grimace as he tried to sit up.

She moved towards him, wanting to take his hand, but not sure she should.

He looked her up and down. "You look like hell."

"I didn't sleep much last night."

"Why?"

She crossed her arms across her chest. This was not going the way she'd thought it would. "I was worried about you. Coma and all, you know."

"You couldn't sleep because you were worried about me?" He glanced towards the doorway. "From the little bit Aidan said, there was more to it than that."

"He told you?" She turned to glare at the doorway.

"What was he not supposed to tell me?"

She narrowed her eyes. "You said from the little bit he said."

"Yeah. He couldn't explain to me how, you, who don't have a car, weren't here with him and Melody. But when I pressed him on it, he didn't say anything else." His lips pressed together. "I figured you were at Kev's or something."

"What? No!" She shook her head to clear it. "Ah! I forget we haven't talked since that night." She paced the room, trying to figure out where to start.

Finally, she stopped at the end of his bed and stared him down. "Okay. You need to listen and not interrupt. And unless you're literally dying, I'm going to chase any nurse or doctor that tries to come in here out until I've said my piece. Got it?"

"Got it."

"Okay. First, nothing happened between me and Kev. Aidan took him aside as soon as you bolted, told him you had feelings for me, and he avoided me like the plague the rest of the night."

His eyebrows shot up at that, but he stayed silent. A good start.

"Second, when I found out you had feelings for me—I confronted Aidan and forced him to tell me what he'd done, he didn't volunteer the information—I rushed home to tell you that I had feelings for you."

Again that look of surprise, but a slight smile, too.

"But you were gone, you fool." She poked at his good foot for emphasis. "So when I went out there that night in the storm, I had every intention of telling you that I love you."

He lurched upward and fell backward, wincing in pain, his eyes fixed on her face.

"I don't know when it happened, but I want you in my life. Not just as my friend, but as my…everything. When we made love that night—and that's what we did, we didn't just have sex—it was the best night of my life."

"Mine, too."

His gaze was so intense, she trembled as she continued, fighting back tears.

"That scared the hell out of me, you know. I loved Dave. I wanted to be with him forever. But what I felt with you...It was so much more than that."

She took a deep breath. "Melody said something about me being broken open by Dave's death and letting you in more than I'd ever let anyone else in before, blah, blah, blah. Maybe she's right. All I know is all those nights we spent talking...Well, they brought us closer than I'd ever thought possible. And I'm going to be here. I'm not leaving you behind. So you better want me too, because I'm not gonna go easy. You need time, I'll give it to you. But I'm here for the long-haul."

He smiled and she melted under the intensity of the love she saw shining back at her. "I love you, too, Jackie. I wasn't looking for it. I certainly wasn't expecting to feel this way for anyone ever again. But I'm in it for the long-haul, too. Whatever it takes. I'll be there for you." He glanced down at himself. "Even if I have to roll a wheelchair halfway around the world to make it happen, I will."

She moved to his side and kissed him. Gently, softly, letting all the love she felt linger in the space where their lips met.

George ran his good hand through her hair. "I'm sort of disappointed you didn't try to run at least once."

"Well, actually..."

She couldn't look him in the eye as she told him how she'd taken Melody's car, driven all the way to the Auckland airport, checked in for her flight, and only then reconsidered and returned.

But he just laughed and ran a finger down the side of her face with a steady smile.

"I thought you'd be mad."

"No. I'm actually a bit relieved to hear it."

"You are?"

"Tells me what you're feeling is real enough to scare you and not just some temporary sex-induced infatuation."

"No. Definitely not." She kissed him again.

"Good. Because I expect to grow old with you, Jackie. And I'm too old and decrepit to chase you for the rest of my life."

"No need. I'll be right here by your side. Always."

C.K. Carr

She kissed him again, glad she'd come back.

CHAPTER 62

The next week wasn't easy. Jackie spent most of her time at George's side as he slowly recovered from the accident. He had to have two more surgeries on his leg and ended up with an assortment of rods, plates, and screws to hold the bones together. But he didn't lose the leg.

And by the end of the week he was even walking—with a walker and not far, but it was good progress nonetheless.

The head injury had given him yet another scar, but Jackie didn't care. He was still gorgeous to her. It showed all he'd been through. Something she wished were true for her some days.

George came home at the end of the first week, but his recovery was far from over. He struggled daily to make progress while Aidan and Kev covered the charter business and Melody and Jackie did whatever they could to help out.

Over the next few weeks, Jackie and George talked and laughed and planned for their future. They didn't know where they were going to go once he was able to travel, but they'd decided it would be somewhere new to both of them. Somewhere that wasn't full of memories of Nellie or Dave. They flipped through travel sites and talked to friends and dreamed of all the possibilities.

And each night they sat on the porch, Jackie snuggled under George's sheltering arm, listening to the steady beat of his heart, quietly hoping that she'd have a lifetime of nights spent in his arms.

Three weeks after George had come home, he was actually able to walk from his bedroom to the kitchen without a walker or crutch or anyone's help.

To celebrate, Aidan cooked a breakfast that could've fed a small army. There were hash browns, homemade bread, bacon, sausage, waffles, and scrambled eggs filled with feta cheese, tomatoes, and spinach.

They sat around the table, joking and laughing and teasing Aidan about his idea of portion sizes.

Afterwards, Aidan and Melody moved to stand next to one another, holding hands and smiling at each other.

"We have an announcement," Aidan said.

Jackie looked back and forth between them, wondering what it was. Something good; Melody was practically bouncing with excitement.

George looked to her and then back to them. "Well…Out with it. What's up?"

Aidan turned to Melody. "Would you like to do the honors?"

Melody nodded, no longer able to contain herself. "Aidan and I are getting married."

"What?" Jackie almost fell of her chair. "No offense, but I didn't think Aidan was the marrying kind?"

"I wasn't. But…" He took a deep breath and smiled. "If I'm going to be a father, I want to do it right."

"If you're going to be a father? You guys are going to have a kid? Are you pregnant?"

"Not yet." Melody half-shrugged. "But we're going to try."

"We're not just going to try, we're going to succeed," Aidan added.

"Really? What changed your mind?" Jackie realized how rude the question was only after she'd asked it.

"This bloke here." Aidan nodded to George. "Seeing him almost get taken out by a car made me realize that we don't always get forever with the ones we love. And that I didn't want to lose Melody. And..." He shrugged one shoulder. "I don't know. The idea of being a father has sort of grown on me since I started thinking about it."

"That's great. Congratulations!" Jackie hugged them both. "When's the wedding?"

Melody bit her lip. "I figured we'd do it in the States. This also lets us get a visa for Aidan. So maybe six months or so? You'll both be there, won't you?"

"Of course."

"And, uh, we're thinking we might want to settle in Florida. Any chance you two would be interested in going in on a sailing business down that way?"

Jackie looked to George. She definitely would, but would he?

He nodded, smiling at her, his eyes twinkling. "That would be perfect."

Melody clapped her hands. "Great! Lots of details to work out of course, but...yay!" She hugged them both.

CHAPTER 63

That afternoon, Melody and Jackie hiked to the top of a high bluff that allowed them to see for miles along the coastline in either direction. It was a picture-perfect day, the sky a blue so clear and perfect it was unlike anything Jackie had seen anywhere else in the world, birds singing somewhere in the trees nearby, the sun shining.

Jackie worried about George being home alone, but Melody had insisted on dragging her out for a hike whether she wanted to go or not and George had agreed. He said it was good for her to get the exercise and time to talk and relax without caring for his injured ass 24/7.

They sat on weathered tree stumps and ate a lunch of leftover steak and grilled vegetables. No asparagus, sadly. It was so weird to be in a country where you could only get your favorite fruits and vegetables when they were in season even if you were willing to pay for the privilege. She still hadn't gotten used to it.

Melody stared into the distance, her brow slightly furrowed, and sighed softly. She'd been quiet the whole walk.

Jackie kicked her foot. "Out with it. What's wrong?"

"I'm just worried that now that Aidan's agreed to get married and try to have a kid, that I won't be able to."

"Of course you will. You're perfectly healthy. Why wouldn't you?"

"It's not always that easy. I've had three friends get pregnant in the last year and every single one of them had at least one miscarriage first. And one of those friends had to do IVF after multiple miscarriages." She poked at the ground with her foot as she continued. "I have another friend I suspect has given up entirely. And you don't even want to know what it did to her marriage. All that pressure, all those failures..."

Jackie wasn't sure what to say, so she waited for Melody to continue.

"I want this so much, Jackie. But..." She stared at her hands. "But this is just the start of what could be a very long, very stressful process. And I don't know how Aidan will handle it."

"You can't think like that."

"I'd rather think like that and be prepared for the worst, than assume it's all going to be fine and find out it isn't. And..." She clenched and unclenched her hands. "I'm scared. Now that he said yes, I want this so much. To see Aidan holding our child in his arms... But I can't make it my world. Because if it doesn't happen I can't let that ruin what we do have."

Jackie nodded. "You're right. You're so happy right now. Hold onto that for as long as you can."

"You don't think I'm ruining things do you? By wanting it all?"

Jackie did wonder if Aidan was the type to be a good settled down father. But she wasn't about to tell Melody that. Not if he'd said he was willing to do it. "No. Why shouldn't you want it all?"

Melody nodded nervously. "Good. Thank you."

They fell into silence as they both ate their food and stared out at the beautiful day.

Jackie's mind drifted towards George, wondering if someday they'd have a baby, too. She thought she'd like that. And that he'd be a good father. She could picture him, running around with their kid on his shoulders, both of them smiling and laughing…

It would be good.

Someday.

When they were settled and ready to make that next step…

She set her food down and stood up.

"Jackie? You okay?"

"Yeah. I'm fine…I just…" She just hadn't had her period since that first night with George. She hadn't thought anything about it. Right after Dave died she'd been all over the place. Early, late, non-existent. But she'd started to settle back into her steady-as-a-clock, every-thirty-days rhythm. Hadn't been off the last six months.

Until now. Could it be? Was she pregnant? She didn't feel pregnant. But…

C.K. Carr

Was she?

She had to find out. She tried to sound casual as she asked, "Do you mind if we run by the store on the way home? I need to pick something up."

"Sure. No problem."

CHAPTER 64

It wasn't exactly easy to hide from Melody what she was doing. Jackie had tried to get her to wait in the car, but she'd insisted on coming in. She wanted to make a cake for their last big meal together. So Jackie had had to make up some ridiculous excuse about needing a few personal items and then almost been caught out when Melody finished her shopping faster than she'd expected and joined her in the checkout line.

But she thought she'd pulled it off without Melody noticing. She'd thrown a bunch of other crap in there just to divert suspicion.

Either that or Melody was polite enough to keep it to herself.

C.K. Carr

As soon as they arrived home, Jackie rushed to the bathroom with the little box. She'd been too scared to buy the ones with the lines and pluses and whatever and had instead settled for the one that literally said, "pregnant" or "not pregnant".

No confusion there, she figured.

It felt like an eternity as she paced her room, waiting for the time to elapse from peeing on the stick to result. She could hear Melody and George talking in the living room. She wondered what they'd both say. Her friend who was worried she might never get pregnant and the man she loved who surely wasn't expecting to have kids almost immediately.

It was time.

She looked at the stick.

Pregnant.

There it was, one little word, black on a white background. She was pregnant.

She sat down on the bed, not knowing what to think or feel.

She'd always told herself that if she did end up pregnant, she'd keep it. She had the financial means and didn't believe in tempting fate like that. Choose not to have a kid now and who knows if she'd ever get the chance again?

She fully supported any other woman's choice on that kind of thing, but for her there'd never been any doubt. Worst case scenario, she'd always figured she'd go it alone. Hire an au pair to help out and make it work.

But now there was George.

And she didn't want to lose him.

What would he say? Would he want her to keep it? Would he stay with her?

And if he didn't? What would she do then?

She loved him. She needed him. But she wanted this child, too. If he made her choose between keeping the baby and staying with him, what would she do?

CHAPTER 65

That night, as she sat on the porch with him, sheltered under his strong arm, looking out at yet another perfect night, she told him about her conversation with Melody. "She's so worried she won't be able to get pregnant and that it'll stress their relationship. And I can see that. But I'm honestly more worried that maybe Aidan is being forced into this whole husband and father role and won't like it. And then what?"

"It's a hard transition to make. Especially for men like Aidan. To go from sailing around, seeing the world, to suddenly anchored in one spot with more and more responsibilities attaching themselves to you like barnacles."

She stared at their entwined fingers. Even though what she felt for George seemed as solid as an oak tree, she sometimes wondered if it was actually more like a soap bubble, so fragile it might burst at the slightest touch.

If it did, she'd shatter into a hundred million jagged pieces that could never be put back together again.

"And you." She turned to look at him, feeling the chill where his body had warmed hers. "Are you going to be okay settling down in Florida?"

"Absolutely."

"You won't miss it? A new country every season?"

He shook his head. "Nah. I had a good run. But...Nice and stable is pretty appealing to me right now. Especially if I have you by my side."

She chewed on her thumbnail "And what about kids? Do you think you'd want them someday?"

She pictured him cradling a tiny little child in his arms, singing it softly to sleep, bringing that same steady love to fatherhood that he'd brought to their relationship.

She couldn't look at him. She didn't know what she'd do if he said no.

"Jackie? Look at me, please."

She swallowed and looked at him, struggling not to immediately look away again.

He held her gaze, his green eyes intense but steady. "I know it's early for us. Probably too early to think of these things."

"Yeah, it is too early, isn't it?" She tried to pull her hand out of his, but he held on.

"But..." He held her gaze. "If you ever want to have a child with me, I can't think of something I'd want more. I'll understand if you never do. And I'll still love you no matter what. But if you want to be a mother, I'd love to be the father of your child."

She felt the tears gathering in her eyes and tried to hold them back, but she couldn't. He pulled her close and held her as she struggled to get herself together.

When she'd finally stopped crying he wiped the tears from her cheeks and asked, "Are you okay now? What did I say?"

She took a deep breath. "I hope you meant what you said just now."

"Of course, I did. I wouldn't have said it otherwise. Why?" His eyes widened as it started to dawn on him. "You're pregnant."

"I am." She bit her lip, waiting for him to pull away, to freak out and say he hadn't really meant it.

Instead, he pumped the air with his fist and let out a loud whoop. "Really?"

"Yes. I took the test just now. I mean, we'll have to go to the doctor to confirm, but…yeah."

"This is great!" He kissed her hard on the lips.

"You're sure?"

"Aren't you?"

"Yes, but…"

He held her face between his two strong hands. "Jackie, I love you. And I can't imagine anything better than bringing a child that's the best of you and the best of me into this world."

She felt that last little fear and hesitation melt away under his strong gaze.

"Oh, this is so great." He kissed her once more. "Can you imagine…"

As he painted a picture of their future, a little boy and a little girl running around their boat shop as he sailed and she helped run the store, she snuggled under his arm and let herself dream of the wonderful life they were going to have.

It wasn't going to be perfect or easy, life never was. But it didn't matter.

Because she'd have George there right beside her. He'd given her back everything she'd lost and more. She would've never believed three months ago that she could find a love that matched the one she'd shared with Dave.

But she had.

It didn't negate that first love—nothing could erase those wonderful memories or change the love they'd shared. But this...

What she had with George...

This was a love to grow old with.

And she'd treasure every single moment they had together. Because she knew how precious a gift it was too have found a love like this a second time.

EPILOGUE:
THREE MONTHS LATER

Jackie ran up the porch steps and into the house, calling back to George, "Hey, come on, Aidan and Melody are supposed to be calling any minute now."

It was colder now—almost the middle of winter—but today had been a gorgeous day for them to get out on the beach for a nice, long walk. George made his steady way up the steps. His leg was still stiff, and probably always would be, but he'd thrown himself into rehab and was doing better than anyone had expected.

The computer started to ring with a Skype call and Jackie managed to answer it just in time. "Hey guys!" she said as she seated herself at the breakfast bar.

"Hey!" Melody and Aidan chimed in unison, pressed close together so they were both visible.

They'd called every single week since they'd left, checking in on George and Jackie, making sure they were still alright. Jackie missed them. Maybe not living **with** them, although she did miss Aidan's cooking, but living near them, at least.

George came to join her, waving at the screen as he settled into a chair next to Jackie's.

"You guys are looking good," Melody said.

"Feeling good, too. We just got back from a walk along the beach. Only chance all day before it starts raining."

"Good. Because we have news!" Melody's grin was so big it practically split her face in half.

"What is it?" Jackie asked.

"We're pregnant!" Melody beamed at Aidan and he smiled back at her, both glowing with the news.

"Congratulations! That's wonderful. How far along are you?"

"Six weeks, so it's still early days."

"That was fast!"

Melody smirked at Aidan. "Aidan says we had such an easy time of it because it was his super Irish sperm at work."

"What can I say?" He shrugged, clearly proud of himself.

Jackie shook her head. "Honestly, Aidan."

George leaned close and whispered in her ear. "Should we tell them? Aren't going to be able to hide it much longer anyway."

"I guess we could," she whispered back, chewing on her thumbnail.

"What are you two whispering about? Out with it." Melody narrowed her eyes.

"Just that..." Jackie looked to George. She couldn't help smiling. She'd wanted to tell Melody from the start but hadn't wanted to upset her since she was trying to get pregnant herself. "Well...We're pregnant, too!"

"What? Oh my god, that's wonderful! Okay, now we really need to get this Florida thing up and running pronto. Can you imagine? The four of us running a little sailing business, maybe living in houses that are next door to one another..."

Jackie laughed. "Or down the street from one another, perhaps?"

"No. Definitely next door. As long as you two don't go running around naked in your backyard…"

"No promises there." George winked at her.

"Oh, well then…"

As they bantered back and forth about what it might be like to be neighbors, Jackie couldn't help but smile. She rested a hand against her belly and leaned into George's embrace, picturing a future she would've never thought possible less than a year ago. She'd lost so much. And as hard as that had been, she was grateful for where she'd ended up.

And for all she'd gained.

If you haven't already read it, check out **Something Worth Having** to see how Melody and Aidan first got together.

ABOUT THE AUTHOR

C.K. Carr likes to write about when love is complicated and messy. Like they say, write what you know.

You can reach her at callistacarr@gmail.com.

Printed in Great Britain
by Amazon